Also by Luiz Alfredo Garcia-Roza

Alone
in the Crowd

Alone
in the Crowd

AN INSPECTOR ESPINOSA MYSTERY

Luiz Alfredo
GARCIA-ROZA

Translated by Benjamin Moser

Henry Holt and Company
New York

Henry Holt and Company, LLC
Publishers since 1866
175 Fifth Avenue
New York, New York 10010
www.henryholt.com

Henry Holt ® and ® are registered trademarks of
Henry Holt and Company, LLC.

Originally published in Brazil in 2007 under the title
Na Multidão by Companhia das Letras, São Paulo

Library of Congress Cataloging-in-Publication Data
García-Roza, L. A. (Luiz Alfredo)
[Na Multidão. English]
Alone in the crowd : an Inspector Espinosa mystery / Luiz Alfredo Garcia-Roza ;
translated by Benjamin Moser.—1st U.S. ed.
    p. cm.—(Inspector Espinosa mysteries)
Originally published in Brazil in 2007 under the title Na Multidão.
ISBN-13: 978-0-8050-7959-3 (alk. paper)
ISBN-10: 0-8050-7959-9 (alk. paper)
  1. Detectives—Brazil—Fiction. 2. Brazil—Fiction. I. Moser, Benjamin.
II. Title.
PQ9698.17.A745N313   2009
869.3'42—dc22   2008050135

First U.S. Edition 2009

Printed in the United States of America
1   3   5   7   9   10   8   6   4   2

The original social content of the crime novel is
every individual's loss of bearings amid the big-
city crowd.

—WALTER BENJAMIN

The essence of all crime is undivulged.

—EDGAR ALLAN POE

Alone

in the Crowd

With one hand, the woman pressed her purse to her chest, while with her other hand she clasped a scrap of paper that she glanced at repeatedly. The electronic signboard above the bank tellers' windows at the branch of the Caixa Econômica displayed two numbers: the number of the customer being helped and the number of the window. She'd been sitting among dozens of other retired people and pensioners for more than an hour, waiting her turn. She knew that if she missed her turn she'd have to take another number (this had happened the previous month, when she'd gone to the bathroom). Staying focused on the signboard was especially difficult; she'd been staring at the number on the board and the number in her hand for so long, both had become meaningless. The murmuring of all the people around her bothered her, as did the conversations held close by. She always tried to sit next to someone younger, in case she needed assistance. She feared the elderly, solitary people who spoke of abandonment in monotonous voices. They disturbed her concentration.

"One seventy-two," said the woman in the next chair, turning toward her.

She looked at the paper and raised her hand. Shouting wouldn't help. Nor did they pay attention to her raised arm. She got up from where she was and rushed to the counter, where the teller called out the number once again and got ready to press the button that would summon the next customer, condemning her to having to take another number.

"It's hard to get through with all these people around," she told him breathlessly.

"All you have to do is wait close to the counter when the number ahead of yours is called," the teller said. "Your card, please."

She had temporarily forgotten the other reason she was there. She opened her purse and started looking for her Social Security card. For an hour and a half she'd been paying such close attention to the numbers that flashed on the screen and the number on the paper she held in her hand. She hadn't thought about the card.

"Next time, ma'am, please come with your card ready. You're holding up other people."

"Everyone who comes here knows they're going to be held up.... They already know they've lost their entire morning or afternoon."

"So what are you complaining about?"

"I'm not complaining. I've been waiting for an hour and a half without saying a word. Here's my card."

"Are you going to withdraw all of it?"

"Yes."

While she counted the money, she looked around as if afraid that someone was about to approach her.

Around a hundred people, eager to get to their business with the bank, were looking at her, but nobody could hear what she was saying. She counted the money once again and handed it back to the cashier, who counted it in turn. Finally, he removed a few more banknotes from a drawer, adding them to the stack he handed back to her.

Back home, she didn't change clothes. She fixed a light meal and watched the TV news while she ate. Later, as soon as the midday heat started to let up, she planned to go out again, to the pharmacy and the supermarket. She also planned to stop by the police station. She'd lived on the same street, in the same building, for more than thirty years, and for the first time she thought she had a reasonable motive for going there.

At five o'clock, after making the trip to the pharmacy and the supermarket and still pushing her shopping cart, the pensioner walked through the gateway to the two-story building of the Twelfth Precinct in Copacabana and encountered the two or three steps that led to the reception area. After crossing that obstacle, she entered a police station for the first time, a bit disappointed. She had expected to find an intensely active and smoky environment, smelling of sweat and cigarettes, uniformed policemen dashing through with men in handcuffs, telephones ringing off the hook, people shouting. She didn't see anyone in uniform, or shouting, or handcuffed. She was greeted by a friendly girl in a setting that reminded her more of a post office than the police stations she'd seen in American movies.

"May I help you?" the girl said.

"Is this the police station?"

"Yes, ma'am."

"Where are all the policemen?"

"Almost everyone who works here is a policeman, ma'am. Would you like to speak to anyone in particular?"

"I'd like to speak with the chief."

"He's in a meeting."

"Will it take long?"

"He's meeting with his team. It usually takes a while. Would you like to speak to Detective Welber, his assistant?"

"It's not the same thing. . . . Is that detective a foreigner?"

"No, ma'am, he's Brazilian."

"Welber . . ."

"The name sounds foreign, but he's Brazilian. You'll like talking to him."

"It doesn't matter whether I'd like to talk to him, sweetheart, it's that I'd like to talk to someone more experienced."

"Detective Welber is very experienced. But if you don't think he's the right person to talk to, you can speak to Chief Espinosa as soon as the meeting's over."

"Espinosa . . . that's the chief's name?"

"That's right."

"Is he Jewish?"

"Jewish? I don't know. . . . I don't think so. . . .
Would that be a problem?"

"No. Not at all. Just curious."

"Well? What do you prefer, talking to the detective
or waiting for the end of the meeting?"

"I've already spent so much time waiting this morning for my pension at the Caixa Econômica; I just waited
on line at the supermarket to pay for my groceries; I
waited at the pharmacy. . . . I live a block away—I'll go
home and drop off these bags and then come back to
speak with the chief."

"Whatever you prefer. What's your name?"

"Laureta Sales Ribeiro."

"You can find me when you come back, Dona
Laureta."

"Thank you. See you in a minute."

It was almost six in the evening by the time Chief
Espinosa ended the meeting with his investigative
team. He hadn't yet left the room when the policeman
on duty came in to say that a woman had been killed
only a block from the station.

"She was here a half hour before—"

"Here at the station?"

"She wanted to talk to the chief."

"Did she know me?"

"No, sir. She just said she wanted to talk to the chief."

"There wasn't anyone available?"

"The receptionist suggested Detective Welber, but she wanted to talk to someone with more experience."

"How was she killed?"

"Run over. She was waiting for the green light to cross the street when she suddenly jerked forward. Some bystanders thought she'd been pushed. She managed to hang on until a fire department ambulance arrived, but she died on the way to the hospital."

"Did she have documents on her?"

"Her purse was filled with documents: address, credit card, health insurance, and money—"

"What was her name?"

"Laureta Sales Ribeiro."

"Did they interview any witnesses?"

"The policemen who got to the scene listened to the people talking about what had happened, but when they called them to testify, the witnesses said that as a matter of fact they hadn't seen anybody push the woman, that they'd just had the impression that she was thrown forward. Vague declarations, mostly from older people who, instead of telling us what they'd actually seen, made long speeches about the violence of the traffic, their fear of being robbed, the war with the drug traffickers, the absence of the police. Nobody felt like coming to the station; they all said that all they'd seen was the woman falling in front of the bus, and even then they couldn't say how she'd fallen or if she'd really been pushed."

"And the bus driver?"

"The only thing he saw was some white hair and then the thud of a body being hit. He was shocked and kept repeating that it wasn't his fault."

A team of investigators spent the rest of the evening retracing Miss Laureta's movements before and after she came to the police station. The accident had occurred during the busiest time of the afternoon, on one of the busiest corners of Copacabana, a few meters from the lobby of the building she lived in and only a block from the Twelfth Precinct.

The receptionist who had talked to Miss Laureta repeated countless times the dialogue she'd had with her. Espinosa wanted her to repeat every word and describe the lady's state of mind: if she seemed scared, anxious, afraid . . .

"She didn't seem like she was any of that. She wasn't scared or frightened. She seemed more anxious than frightened. It didn't seem to be anything too urgent, and she decided herself to come back later. She didn't say anything about what brought her to the station in the first place."

"She might have witnessed some crime, she might have known some incriminating fact, she might have been threatened . . ."

Going on Laureta's comment that she had been at the branch of the Caixa Econômica that morning to collect her pension, Inspector Ramiro and Detective Welber went to the closest branch the next day, three blocks from the station. The only photo they had was the one from the ID card they'd found at the scene of the accident. It was an old picture. It also listed her name. They went from window to window until they found the teller who had helped her. On the badge attached to his shirt were the words HUGO BRENO. He remembered having seen her a few times, and that the day before she had replied a bit harshly to an observation he'd made. He added that he understood the irritation of a senior citizen who had to wait more than an hour to collect what was owed to her. According to him, the only words they had exchanged had to do with the withdrawal she had come to perform.

"She was alone?"

"She was. At least nobody was with her when she came up to the counter."

"Did she seem afraid or scared?"

"No. As I said, she was irritated by the length of the wait."

Espinosa's office, where he learned that Welber's investigation hadn't turned up anything that could help explain the pensioner's death. Ramiro had had no more luck with the employees of her supermarket or the people who worked at the pharmacy or the shops close to her building. There was nothing in Laureta's daily life that pointed to why she would have sought assistance from the police. One aspect of the case did stand out: whatever her reasons for coming to the station, Laureta seemed to be more interested in the chief than in the resources of the station . . . even though she didn't know him personally and didn't even know his name.

"She was probably looking for someone who not only was the boss but whose age she might have imagined was closer to hers," Espinosa said. "She must have thought that the reason she came to the station couldn't be understood by a less experienced policeman. When the receptionist said that Detective Welber had plenty of experience, Laureta insinuated that she wasn't talking about police experience. Another consideration is that she wanted to communicate something important, with regards to herself or to a third party, but she wasn't in a hurry. She may have supposed that nobody knew about the secret she was going to reveal to us. Yet someone did find out, probably on the same day that she was killed. The discovery could have occurred in the morning, in the bank, while she was waiting her turn. Maybe by someone she was talking to and who followed her as

The supermarket and the pharmacy she had visited were evident from the plastic bags found in her apartment, some of which still had her purchases inside. There was no record of any calls made that day from the cell phone found in her purse. They had asked the phone company for a list of the calls she had made from her landline. The doorman remembered that when she went out to the shops she had said that she would pay a visit to the station later.

"That's how she said it, that she'd *pay a visit* to the station later?"

"That's right. I thought it was funny too. Nobody pays a visit to a police station."

By noon the day after the accident, the two policemen had managed to piece together everything Laureta had done from when she'd left home that morning until the moment she was hit, at the end of the afternoon. A few lacunae, like routes and stops, were filled in by Chief Espinosa, in order to create a coherent picture. There was no sign of robbery: in the victim's purse her money, credit card, bank card, checkbook, and cell phone had not been touched. As a few witnesses had said, nobody saw her being pushed, if in fact she had been; what they did see was the sudden movement of her body. There was no exclamation. Nobody ran off. There was no strange activity: she simply threw herself, or was thrown, forward, as vehicles were moving swiftly past.

"There's nothing that points to a motive," Ramiro said. "She was a widow who lived alone, surviving modestly on her husband's pension, a peaceful lady who didn't have any problems with anyone."

"But nobody is thrown in front of a bus in broad daylight on a street corner densely packed with pedestrians, without anyone seeing a thing," Espinosa observed. "According to what our receptionist said, suicide is very improbable; we have to take into consideration the possibility that she was pushed. And we're only going to discover someone's motive for doing that when we find out what she was planning on saying here at the station a half hour before she died."

In the afternoon, Chief Espinosa put Welber in charge of talking to the employees who worked in Laureta's building and with the other people who lived on her floor. Espinosa thought that a widowed lady living by herself, without a maid, would tend to chat to certain people about her day-to-day life. Some of those facts might have something to do with what happened to her. Welber started with the neighbors. There were three apartments on her floor, besides her own. The one immediately next to hers belonged to a couple of landowners from Minas Gerais who kept the apartment for their occasional visits to Rio, roughly every two months—and they hadn't been there for more than a month. Of the other two apartments, one belonged to a very elderly man who was suffering from senility and

was attended to by two assistants, who took care of him in shifts. They knew Laureta only by sight. They hadn't even heard that she had been run over.

"There is some doubt about whether it was an accident," Welber mentioned to one of the assistants.

"What do you mean, someone killed the old lady?"

"Possibly. . . . And she wasn't just an old lady. It was a woman who was still fairly strong."

"We hardly ever saw her. Every once in a while we'd run into each other in the elevator and say hello. Nothing more than that."

The third apartment housed two girls. They worked in a real-estate office and spent every day, including Saturdays and Sundays, away from home. Welber managed to talk to one of them at the real-estate office; she had nothing noteworthy to add, even though she remembered her neighbor.

The building's employees, a few doormen and a janitor, sometimes received calls from Laureta, with requests to change a light bulb or to fix something. At these times, they sometimes would chat, but never about anything that suggested a threat or a particular concern. Laureta only had one girlfriend, whom Welber met, an acquaintance left over from the time when their husbands were alive and the couples spent time together. She was deeply shocked by the news of her friend's death. She had no idea why such a thing might have happened.

At the end of the afternoon, the team

soon as she left the bank. In the afternoon, after she'd gone to the supermarket and the pharmacy, she entered the station, and the stalker got scared, thinking she was going to turn him in, but he must have been relieved when she was in here for only a short time. Because of her calm demeanor as she walked out, he must have thought that she hadn't talked yet. That's when he decided to kill her as soon as possible."

Only Inspector Ramiro and Detective Welber were with Espinosa in his office. It was starting to get dark when the chief gave them their assignments for the next day.

"What I've just told you is nothing more than a vague suspicion without any real basis, of course, but it's all we've got for now. I want you to go back to the bank, examine the tapes from the security cameras, see who was sitting next to her, who she was talking to, who came up to her, if she went to the bathroom, if someone followed her . . . everything. . . . I want you to examine every second she spent inside that bank. And also outside it. See if there are cameras on the sidewalk in front of the agency. Another thing: the cashier who helped her must have been at a window in front of the chairs where people sit waiting their turn. The retirees and pensioners always get their money in the same branch and are almost always assisted by the same teller, who ends up knowing them by sight. Maybe the teller saw Laureta being approached by some stranger. . . . Anyway . . . look for anything that might indicate a more concrete instigator than the suppositions I've just made."

"Why do you think this was more likely to happen in the bank and not in the supermarket, the pharmacy, or somewhere else?" Welber asked.

"It could have happened anywhere, of course. I just think it's more likely to have happened in the bank. That's where she spent the most time, she was in contact with more people, it was easier for her to recognize people and to be recognized herself. In other words, someone waiting like that is more likely to pay attention to what's going on around them than someone who's in the aisles of a supermarket or a pharmacy doing their shopping. What the murderer couldn't do was kill her in the bank or even in the supermarket. In both places he'd be easily taken down by the security guards. He preferred to follow her during the day and wait for a better moment—when she went back home in the afternoon, for example. But when he saw her go into the station and leave ten minutes later, he didn't think he could wait any longer. What we've got on our side is that he doesn't know if she managed to tell us anything before she left."

It was seven at night when Espinosa left the station thinking about passing through the Galeria Menescal to buy some meatballs and pies. From what he remembered of the night before, the only item left in his refrigerator was half of a lasagna that no longer was at the peak of its tastiness. The Arab reinforcements were not meant to be added to the half lasagna but were intended as substitutes, a break from the monotony of the last few days of eating frozen pasta. Lately, he'd been thinking about eliminating dinner. Just that. Decreeing the end of dinner. And therefore decreeing the end of frozen pastas. He'd start eating a little snack: café au lait, black bread, cheese, ham, jelly . . . something lighter, healthier, less fattening, more appropriate to the tropical climate (though he wasn't quite sure why), less laborious (he wasn't sure if that was actually the case), and, finally, a more American and European evening meal (or so he thought). While he walked, he thought about it. The meatball option actually seemed like a compromise: it wasn't frozen pasta and it wasn't coffee. Still, the very idea of a snack instead of a dinner sounded more like a capitulation than a change. He'd felt older ever since the idea occurred to him. . . . Or was he feeling older and that was why the idea had occurred to him? Would the next step be wearing house slippers?

The route through the Galeria Menescal wasn't the shortest path to the Peixoto District, where Espinosa lived, but it was still his favorite. When he was a boy, he got off the bus on his way back from school on the Avenida Copacabana, in front of the Galeria Menescal—

which also serves as a passageway linking the Avenida Copacabana to the Rua Barata Ribeiro on his way back to the Peixoto District. Even now, as an adult, the enormous gateway flanked by marble columns felt imposing. When he was a boy, before he started walking through, he would stop in the gateway and look up, enraptured by the incredibly high ceiling and the sequence of shops on both sides, with the smaller, odder stores above them. Still a boy, he had been fascinated by the story that because it had been built during the war, the gallery's underground garage contained a reinforced area that could serve as an air-raid shelter. Though the war had ended almost two decades before Espinosa's birth, the boy felt a special importance in walking through an air-raid shelter. Halfway through the gallery, absorbed by adventure stories from World War II, he made his customary stop in the Arab take-out place to buy either meatballs or meat pies (one day the one, one day the other) to feed his boyish hunger and the imagination of the future Chief Espinosa.

The difference was that on that Tuesday he wasn't coming back from school happily anticipating the passageway and his stop at the Arab restaurant. He was coming from the Twelfth Precinct, of which he was the chief, thinking sadly about what had led Laureta to come looking for him at the end of the afternoon on which she died without being able to speak to him. He walked slowly through the gallery, hands in his pockets, eyes cast downward. Seen from a distance, he stood out from the rest of the crowd because of his above-average height and the almost imperceptible swaying of his upper body, which recalled the motion of a metronome. He went into the little shop without hesitating. He ordered two meatballs and two pies.

2

Amid the compact mass of pedestrians moving slowly
down the sidewalk like a giant centipede, the man had
the feeling that these weren't people walking but that
their legs really belonged to that big urban animal that
drags itself heavily through the streets of large cities. Yet
that didn't bother him. He liked crowds, he just didn't
think that now was the right time to enjoy them. At six-
thirty that evening he had to be in the bar in front of
the Twelfth Precinct, on the Rua Hilário de Gouveia,
and it was already past six. That wouldn't have been a
problem with the flow of pedestrian traffic at any other
hour of the day, but with the movement on the sidewalks
at that hour on the Avenida Copacabana, of people getting off work and the still-bustling shops, the morose-
ness with which the crowd was moving posed an obstacle
to anyone who was in a hurry. He was about to find an
easier route when some traffic light somewhere up
ahead liberated the flux of people and the block started
moving a bit more briskly. Nothing out of the ordinary,
but enough of a release to allow him to go down that
one block a little quicker. The man let himself be carried along for a little ways in the same rhythm as the
crowd, but then he had to get off the sidewalk to speed
up, walking between the curb and the cars.

It was a good choice. Ten minutes later, he was drinking a coffee at the bar in front of the station. He stood at the counter, drinking unhurriedly, watching the people who were going through the doorway of the Twelfth Precinct. He wanted to stay for only a short while, so as not to draw attention to himself. After fifteen minutes, he started walking toward Barata Ribeiro, no more than fifty feet away. The traffic, at that hour, was intense. He crossed the street and stood in front of the window of the shop on the corner, still keeping an eye on the people entering and leaving the station. At seven, he saw the chief come out onto the sidewalk, take a left, and head down the street toward the corner where he was standing. He walked at a leisurely pace, as if mulling something over, without any apparent direction. The man waited to see if the chief would turn onto Barata Ribeiro or if he would keep going all the way to the Avenida Copacabana. He kept going. Even better. From that point on, he could guess where the chief would go. He kept a safe distance until they turned right onto the Avenida Copacabana, at which point, thanks to the number of pedestrians, he could get closer without risking notice, though the chief didn't seem interested in what was going on around him anyway. After walking two and a half more blocks, they entered the Galeria Menescal, where the crowd of people thinned. About halfway through the gallery, the chief's gait slowed and he entered the little Arab restaurant, apparently without giving conscious thought to what he was doing. The man knew that the policeman wouldn't stay longer than was necessary to buy a snack. The shop was full, with people constantly entering and leaving. He himself went in and ordered, just like the chief: a couple of meatballs and a pie.

The two left the shop almost simultaneously, after the chief greeted the cashier, the restaurant's owner. Because the chief was still walking slowly and reflexively, the man overtook him and made his way through the gallery, leaving him behind. He wasn't planning to stalk Chief Espinosa wherever he went but just to enjoy the secret pleasure of being side by side with him, and even to buy and savor the same Arab delicacies. On Barata Ribeiro, he walked another half block back to Siqueira Campos, almost completing a perfect rectangle since leaving the station. He walked down the street with a firm stride, without looking behind him or to the sides. Unconcerned with the intense pedestrian traffic, he passed the subway station and the cutoff between Siqueira Campos and the Ladeira dos Tabajaras and in the space of a few minutes entered his building, an older construction, small and only three stories high, with one apartment on every floor. He went straight to his room, the same one that for years had been his mother's, and opened the window to let the hot air that had gathered in the course of the afternoon circulate. The furniture was all the same. Not even the dressing table had been removed. The bed, which his mother had called her widow's bed and which now was his, was in the same place, in front of the old wardrobe. The only fixtures he'd added to the room were a full-length mirror, attached to the only free wall, and a gymnastic bar he'd installed in the doorway. He took off his clothes and stood in his underwear. He looked at himself from the front, the sides, and the back. He wasn't tall, he wasn't good-looking, but he was strong, agile, without any excess fat. He had light eyes, a brown crew cut, and he was meticulously careful with the cleanliness of his body. He did two sets of sit-ups and push-ups and a set of repetitions on the bar. He showered, put on some shorts, and turned on the television. He hadn't had dinner. He remembered the package he'd left on the living-room table. All he had in the refrigerator was milk, two slices of bread, and a piece of cheese, along with a can of soda. His purchases from the Arab restaurant completed his meal.

He was satisfied with his tailing of Chief Espinosa. He didn't expect anything more than that, and that was enough for now. He was more and more convinced that he and the chief had some things in common. They were more or less the same age (he was a year younger), both were public employees, lived alone, had lived in the same neighborhood since childhood (only two blocks away from each other), and they both liked to walk through Copacabana. Maybe he should have also said that neither of them had been very sociable— since childhood. So that might have been why they never became friends. While he was eating his meatballs, he thought he could add another similarity between them: their taste for Middle Eastern food. He imagined the chief seated next to his living-room window, looking in the direction of his building at that exact same moment, also eating the food he'd bought at the same restaurant. He knew that most evenings the chief ate alone. Only on Fridays did he have the company of a woman, much younger than he was and really pretty, who arrived carrying grocery bags. It was always the same one, his girlfriend for years, who'd never moved in with him (he certainly would have noticed if she had). On Friday nights, they seemed to linger longer over their dinner. He'd never seen the inside of the chief's apartment, but when the French windows were open you could see his living room from the square. It was definitely much bigger than the man's. Moreover, the chief's entire apartment was definitely bigger and nicer than his. But that didn't bother him. He wasn't interested in things like furniture, decoration, and art objects. He didn't think the chief was either, since they had so many other things in common. Although, of course, this didn't apply to the chief's luck with women, which he didn't have.

On certain Friday nights, especially in the summer, he liked to sit on a bench in the square and watch Espinosa and his girlfriend move around the living room. He couldn't see much of them, except when they came all the way up to the balcony beside the French windows, which was rare. He wouldn't like to be with them, since that was an intimate moment between two lovers, but he would have loved to be able to lean over that balcony beside the chief and enjoy, with him, the opposite view to the one he had when he was sitting on the park bench.

All he'd eaten was the meatballs, and he'd drunk the soda. The rest of the meal would have to be eaten with milk, the only drink he had left, besides water. He didn't drink alcohol or smoke. Not for moral or religious reasons, but because they were bad for your health. He wasn't religious and he didn't believe in God; he didn't have relatives or friends. That's why he took such care with his body and mind. If one of the two let him down, he wouldn't have anyone to turn to. And even if he did, he wouldn't have turned to them. He cleaned the table, washed the few dishes he'd used, and turned on the television, which he'd turned off when the news was about to start. He didn't like TV news, and he was particularly repulsed by comedy programs. He especially liked when they played films, because then he didn't have to leave his house, and also because of the pleasure of watching a film without anyone sitting on all sides of him, talking or bumping into him, eating popcorn or sucking on the straw in their soda. On TV, it wasn't so much the films he was interested in as the absence of people making him uncomfortable from every side. He did like to read, but he didn't accumulate books. He bought them in used-book stores and got rid of them as soon as he was done with them. He'd even sold off his mother's books as soon as she died. He didn't like music, either popular or classical. The only sound equipment he had at home was a little battery-powered radio that had belonged to his mother. He thought he himself was enough to fill his life satisfactorily. Hookers were more than enough for his sexual needs. The world wasn't complicated in the least. Sometimes there were little problems, which he overcame or solved without much trouble.

The next morning, on his way to work, the man thought of something else he had in common with Chief Espinosa: both of them worked only a few blocks away from where they lived, and their routes to work were almost the same. But he was sure that the chief had never realized that. If they'd passed each other on the street or even walked side by side on their way to work or back home—and both things had happened— the chief wouldn't have noticed or cared, simply because he didn't remember him. They didn't keep the same hours. The chief's schedule was irregular; sometimes he didn't leave the office until late at night, whereas he spent other days entirely away from the station. But despite this, they did occasionally cross paths in one of the predictable trips to and from work or even just walking through the neighborhood, something both enjoyed doing. Their strides were distinct: his was firm, hurried, almost military, while the chief's was slow, distracted, as if his thoughts were wandering off, miles away.

When he got to the branch of the Caixa Econômica, minutes before the beginning of his shift, there was already a line of senior citizens waiting for the door to open in order to get their numbers. By one in the afternoon, when he took his lunch break, the policemen he'd seen the day before hadn't appeared. And there was no reason for them to. There was nothing else to say about it except repeat the words he'd exchanged with the pensioner, all of which he'd already reported to the policemen who had come looking for him. The woman had certainly told them that she'd been in the bank that morning. But besides repeating the conversation between the two, conceding that it was perhaps a bit prickly, all he could have added was that she'd recognized him, since she visited the branch at least once a month. Yes, he would insist if they asked him again, she was nervous, a bit irritated, but that was natural enough, since there were so many people there that day and on the days when pensions were paid out the elderly pensioners had to wait a long while before being helped. Besides, they were slow, they forgot their paperwork, they got distracted and missed their number. When their turn finally came, they were annoyed and complained to the cashier. But just like all the other cashiers, he was used to it. There was no reason the cops would come back looking for him.

So he was surprised when he saw the two arrive, right when he was about to go back to work. He hadn't even managed to reopen his window or press the button to call the next customer. He waited for them to come over.

"Good morning, sir. I'm Inspector Ramiro and this is Detective Welber. We were here yesterday."

"I remember you."

"We came in the afternoon today so as not to interfere with the customers."

"That, unfortunately, is impossible. Especially during the first few days of the month, one less cashier does make a difference."

The policemen showed their IDs to the security staff and went behind the window.

"It's better for us to talk over here, so they won't think we're breaking in line."

"Aren't you, though?"

"True enough, but we're not going to be long. We just want to clear up a few details. On Monday morning, when you were helping the pensioner Laureta Sales Ribeiro, you were working at this same window?"

"Yes. Whenever possible, we stay in the same place."

"So you could see exactly what we can see from here."

"Exactly."

"And according to what you told us, Laureta was sitting in the third row."

"That's right. In the middle of the third row."

"Was anyone sitting next to her?"

"Yes, on both sides. All the chairs were occupied."

"And was she talking to those people?"

"It's possible, but I wasn't paying attention. I deal with money. I have to be very careful with what I'm doing. But I can tell you that there are two types of senior citizens: the distracted ones, who talk to everyone around and don't even pay attention to see what number's being called, and the other kind, who pay such close attention, who are so focused on their number, that they don't see anything else around them. They don't talk to anyone, and if people are chatting around them they complain. The lady who died was of the second variety. She wasn't one to chat."

"And when you were helping her, she didn't make any comments?"

"The only thing she said is what I already told you."

"Do you mind repeating it?"

"Well, she said that it was hard to get to the counter, with all the people sitting down and standing, blocking her way."

"And what did you say?"

"That she ought to start moving forward as soon as the number before hers was called. Even so, she forgot to take her ID card out of her purse. When I said that she should come up to the counter with her card in her hand, because otherwise she slowed things down, she replied gruffly that whoever came there knew it would

take a long time, sometimes the whole morning. . . .
Something along those lines."

"And did you say anything?"

"I just asked if she was going to withdraw the whole
amount, and she said yes."

"Neither of you said anything else?"

"No."

"Among the people who are waiting now, do you see
anyone who was here on Monday morning?"

"It's hard to say. . . . No . . . I don't remember seeing
any of them on Monday."

"Thanks. We hope we haven't slowed too many
people up."

After that, Welber and Ramiro found the general
manager and the security director to ask for the tapes
from the security cameras that were focused on the
waiting room, as well as those from the front door. With
the help of a photograph taken from the pensioner's
apartment, they spent the rest of the day analyzing the
images the cameras had recorded. Laureta was easily
found. After that, every movement of her head, every
apparent movement of her mouth, as well as those of
the people around her, were noted, as was her visit to the
counter. However, the images of her dialogue with the
cashier were not very clear, because there a grille and a
window stood between them. Moreover, even though
the angle of the camera allowed both parties to be iden-
tified, it was impossible to make out the movement of

their lips with any clarity. But neither her expression nor his movements suggested that either was upset. The images from the sidewalk revealed nothing more than Laureta heading toward the corner.

After his shift, Hugo Breno chose to go home down the Avenida Copacabana. He felt best on the busiest streets, where he could let himself get lost in the crowd. At those times he felt especially at peace with himself and with the world. Sometimes, when there weren't enough people on the street, he went into a large department store and wandered through it without buying anything, just to feel himself surrounded by people. But he did that only when there was nothing else going on: what really attracted him were the giant outdoor masses. When he was among the people in a crowd, he never spoke to anyone and he never looked deliberately at anyone in particular. His participation was silent and solitary. He didn't try to establish relationships or make friends, and he didn't hope for a movement of mass solidarity or for a unifying collective feeling to emerge, some kind of metaphysical "us." He wanted the opposite. He sought out the crowds as a place of multiplicity, not of unity. He wanted singularities, since he himself was one. He didn't want to feel "equal"; he was absolutely attached to being different, to his own uniqueness.

After he left the bank, once the workday was over, he went to the Avenida Copacabana and walked about fifteen blocks. Then he went back to the corner of the Rua Siqueira Campos, at which point he broke off from the pedestrian mass and went back up the street toward his house. He did that almost every day. Not necessarily down the Avenida Copacabana (though he really liked it); sometimes he took the subway all the way downtown (his favorite was the Avenida Rio Branco), walked about ten blocks, and then took the subway back. The experience of the subway at rush hour was the next best thing to the experience of the streets, and sometimes even better.

3

It was Friday and Espinosa had arranged a dinner with Irene. She'd just gotten in from São Paulo, where she'd been working for two weeks. It was one of the longest periods they'd spent apart, not counting the month she'd spent in New York in an intensive course. He was calling her cell phone to confirm.

"Do you mind if someone else comes along?" Irene asked.

"Of course not," he answered, hoping his voice wouldn't let him down.

"Great! Then there will be a surprise guest."

Espinosa would have preferred it to be just the two of them: he hadn't planned on guests. Surely the person would only be eating with them. At least, that's what he hoped.

He walked down Tonelero on his way home, thinking about Irene and how long their relationship had lasted. It was a thought that had been occurring to him more and more. The more time went by, the more obvious the ten years that separated their ages became. Irene had never said it was too much, nor had she ever suggested that it was time to change the nature of their relationship. They had a tacit agreement not to ask the other to get married or to remain sexually faithful. As for their emotional connection itself, they agreed that it didn't need any agreement: either it was real or it wasn't an emotional connection. They also agreed that a relationship doesn't have a backstory: it exists in the present tense, which eliminates any discussions related to earlier times. He was thinking about all this as he crossed the square that was at the center of the Peixoto District, a bit abandoned at that hour, when the kids had been called home for dinner.

He'd arranged to pick up Irene at nine. That was enough time to take a shower, get dressed, call a cab, and get to Ipanema. He'd gotten rid of his old car. It had sat unused for so long in front of his building that the battery died, the tires deflated, and, when he finally got it up and running, it turned out to have a whole range of little mechanical and electrical defects that were the result of its abandonment. They were in the seventh year of the twenty-first century and his car was still from the twentieth. Before it became an antique, he decided to sell it. The term he used to describe the transaction was "get rid of it" instead of "sell." He was very grateful when a guy who lived on the other side of the square agreed to take it off his hands. The price was ridiculously low, so the neighbor was very grateful, too. Everyone was happy. Espinosa was sure that the happiest one of all was his old car, which from then on would lead a dignified life. Not to mention that because it was so close by he could visit it often, though he didn't think the two of them would miss each other. After that trans-action, he had started using taxis for social engagements. For his professional needs, he had the cars from the station.

When the taxi stopped in front of Irene's building, Espinosa got out of the car to greet the two women waiting for him in the lobby. They looked like women of the future. Both very pretty, they looked like each other, despite Irene's friend's blond, short, and upright hair. Irene came up first, hugging and kissing Espinosa.

"Darling, this is Vânia, my friend from São Paulo."

"Hi, Vânia. Welcome."

"Thanks. Irene's told me so much about you."

"Vânia came to spend a week in Rio. She's staying here at my house."

"You couldn't have chosen a better place," Espinosa said.

Vânia was from São Paulo, but she might just as well have been from Berlin, Copenhagen, or New York. Just like Irene, she was a woman from the new millennium, Espinosa thought. He immediately reflected that it was still hard for him to get rid of small but resilient residues of the nineteenth century. They got in the cab and Espinosa gave the driver the address of a little restaurant on the Avenida Atlântica, in Leme, where they could talk quietly.

The three of them were sitting in the back seat. Even though it was a spacious car, their physical proximity promoted an intimacy that was facilitated by the resemblance between the two women. Since they were both in a chatty mood, Espinosa alternatively had one of their arms touching his and one of their legs rubbing up against one of his. It wasn't in the least an unpleasant situation, but when the conversation got more animated, he occasionally got embarrassed, unsure of what to do with his hands. Nineteenth century, he thought.

The trip took them down part of Ipanema Beach and all the way down Copacabana, but it was a straight shot, uncomplicated by traffic. It was enough time for Vânia and Espinosa to start getting along with each other, which didn't seem to bother Irene in the least. During dinner, Vânia expressed interest in Espinosa's work, an interest that he satisfied only minimally but that was enriched by Irene's passionate contributions. The meal was pleasant and could have been perfect except for one question he couldn't shake: What was going to happen afterward? Would Irene and Vânia go back home together and leave him to sleep alone in his apartment, after two weeks spent far apart? Would he and Irene sleep in the Peixoto District, leaving the guest to sleep alone in an apartment she'd hardly had time to see? It didn't seem right or hospitable. There was the "only logical and not real" possibility, he thought, that the three of them would sleep in his own apartment, but that never managed to become a full-fledged thought, just a fleeting and perverse image that crossed his mind and was immediately written off. The dilemma was solved by Irene as they were leaving the restaurant.

"Honey, since it's Vânia's first night here, and since I invited her to stay with me, I'm going to keep her company tonight. Tomorrow and Sunday she's going out with friends who live here in Rio and I'll spend two days with you in your apartment. What do you think?"

"I think it's perfect."

He didn't think it was perfect. Alone in his apartment after dropping the two off in Ipanema, Espinosa thought the solution was perfect according to the rules of hospitality and friendship, but extremely frustrating and unsatisfactory from the point of view of desire.

Reading was out of the question. No text could compensate for the absence of Irene. Television much less, even if he just let the images wash over him. He took off his clothes, lay down in bed, and stared at the ceiling. He understood that Irene didn't have a choice, since she'd invited her friend to stay at her place. What he didn't understand clearly was why the two had planned it beforehand—since there was no doubt that they'd planned it. And it didn't mean any suffering for Irene, or at least not that she showed. Of course she wasn't suffering for being with her friend, and she didn't seem to be suffering for not being with him or for leaving him by himself. Or maybe that was it: she preferred to spend her first night in Rio, after two weeks away, in the company of Vânia.

When they met, Irene had just ended a long relationship with a woman, also from São Paulo. Beginning a relationship with him meant, as she herself said, choosing him as a person and as a sexual option. That choice, however, didn't come with promises of heterosexual fidelity. Neither had she promised not to have other homosexual affairs. From what he could tell, Irene's homosexual choices had never excluded heterosexual choices. That was why their involvement had been viable and lasted so long. They'd never brought up the subject again. There was no reason to. What Espinosa was wondering was whether the blond Vânia didn't mean Irene was reverting to her old ways. Or: if that kind of option had ever really stopped existing since they had met or if it still went on, silently, during her trips to São Paulo.

Espinosa got up on Saturday with the strange feeling that he'd been tricked. This, because the first idea that came into his mind was "Today is Saturday," immediately followed by another: "Irene's not here with me," as he stretched his arm out to the side and found nothing but a sheet. The two ideas and the gesture all happened in an instant. He slowly started remembering the conversation the night before, when he'd said good night to Irene, and their agreement to switch Friday night for the entire weekend. From a quantitative perspective, it was doubtless a good trade, but not necessarily gratifying from an emotional point of view. Because they'd been apart for so long, they ought to have stayed together from Friday to Sunday. That was why he felt like he'd been wronged.

He took an almost cold shower, collected the newspapers that his neighbor had been nice enough to leave at his door, and went to make coffee. Saturday mornings had always had a special flavor for him, because on Saturdays there was no limit to the number of pieces of toast he could have or the amount of cheese and jam he could eat, along with two big cups of strong coffee. A problem that persisted to the point of having become almost like a pet, constantly underfoot, was that his toaster browned only one side of the bread at a time, forcing him to carry out the operation in two steps in order to obtain a nice piece of toast. It was an American toaster that dated to the Second World War, inherited from his parents, and that to this day worked magnificently well, except for that little detail. One day, Irene had given him a new toaster as a present, from a top-of-the-line brand. For two weeks the toasters fought it out, side by side, for their owner's favor. On week three, the new toaster was placed in a closet, to await the definitive death of the defective but charming toaster that he made a point of saying dated back to World War II, as if the old machine had fought in the skies above Europe or participated in the naval battles of the Pacific. Irene said that it wasn't the toaster that fed him every morning, but he who fed the toaster, as well as acting as a guardian of its glorious past.

The table was close to the French windows that opened out onto a little balcony of cast iron, and all the windows were open on that luminous Saturday morning. On the weekends, Espinosa also subscribed to the São Paulo papers; he'd started to do that ever since Irene had begun to work regularly in both cities, as if they were simply two different neighborhoods she hung out in. During the week, the news in both papers talked about politics, crime, and economics, but during the weekend there was the compensation of the cultural pages, promising an hour or two of reading, complete with free refills of coffee.

That was the first part of the morning. The second was dedicated to little household duties planned on previous Saturdays or to planning new activities to be carried out on future Saturdays, in case those weren't taken up by planning for other activities. Some of them could be postponed infinitely, whereas others entered the category of "bottomless tasks," which placed them in limbo (even though that celestial waiting room had been declared nonexistent by the church). That was the case, for example, with the project of constructing wooden shelving to house the books that were piled up all along one wall of the living room, in a heap that for him had acquired the status of a work of art and that would give way to conventional shelving only once it had collapsed all over the room, which he could guarantee would never happen. Ever since he began living on his own, especially since the death of his grandmother, from whom he'd inherited many of the books there, Espinosa used what he called provisional shelving: he'd chosen the longest wall in the room and started piling his books up there, from the floor up, one row of books standing up, upon which he'd deposited a sequence of books lying flat, like a first shelf, upon which he'd lined up another row of standing books, covered by another series of books lying flat, and so on and so forth, in a rising construction whose limit would obviously be the ceiling. That's what he started calling his "shelf-less shelving" or "shelving in the purest state" or "a shelf made only out of books," and now, a few decades on, it took up the entire wall of the living room and was more than six feet tall . . . and hadn't fallen over once.

But the main promise of that morning was Irene's arrival for a weekend with just the two of them. They'd arranged to meet for lunch, which would give him time to tidy up the apartment and to order the best sushi and sashimi combination from his favorite Japanese restaurant. For him, that was the ideal food for a lunch that would lead to predictable, and desirable, activities afterward.

Tidying up the apartment had nothing to do with the obsessive competence of the maid who came once a week; it just meant cleaning off the countertops, taking out the trash, and making the bed. Sometimes it also included gathering up the books he'd left on chairs, tables, and even the floor, near the rocking chair where he liked to read.

When Irene arrived, the only reason she wasn't greeted with candles lit on the table was that it was lunchtime and not dinner; it was only about one and it was so bright outside that they almost needed sunglasses inside the house. She arrived looking pretty and happy.

"I brought two bottles of white wine to go with our lunch, even though I didn't know what we were having. I have to put them in the fridge."

Their embrace was intense, longing, charged with their pasts. There was a time when after not seeing each other for a while they'd hugged passionately, breathlessly, overflowing with desire. That was back when Irene climbed the stairs of the building announcing from the first steps what she'd brought with her and expressing out loud what a delight she herself was. That was when her absences were rarely longer than two or three days. Now, after two weeks apart, their embrace was still full of desire, happiness, intensity, but it also had a memory. Also in their sexual encounters, there was, more than the intimacy of the bodies they explored so minutely, the mutual intimacy those bodies had experienced through the time they'd been together. It was no longer a question of quantity versus quality, nor a substitution of one for the other, but a heightening of intensity: something made of quantity and quality that couldn't be reduced to one or the other.

Espinosa was thinking about those questions dizzily while he and Irene embraced and exchanged their first few words, even though he realized that what he was thinking was only his own point of view. What did Irene think about that? How was she seeing him today? Had things improved or gotten worse? Maybe both. He didn't know. He noticed how they took off their clothes slowly, without impatience.

The contact between their bodies wasn't hurried either.

"Sorry I left you alone last night."

"I don't think you had a choice."

"I did. . . . But it would have been hard for her."

"It was also hard for me."

"I could have let her figure it out by herself."

"If you didn't it's because you couldn't."

"Now you're being mean."

"No, I'm not. You're feeling guilty. If after sex you turn to me and say you're sorry for not sleeping with me last night, the reason is that you could have. You didn't because you preferred to sleep with your friend."

"I don't understand the ambiguity."

"The verb 'sleep with' has a double meaning."

"You mean you think I'm having an affair with Vânia?"

"Baby, if I wanted to say that, I would have. . . . You're the one who just said it."

"I didn't say it, I asked."

"I'm not the one you have to ask that question."

"Espinosa, what's going on with you? I hardly recognize you."

"But I'm afraid I do recognize you."

"Damn it! What's gotten into you?"

"Listen: you tell me you spent two weeks in São Paulo working with Vânia and staying in her apartment. Which means you were with her night and day. Once the work is done, you come to Rio with her and let her stay in your house. Vânia is a very pretty woman, sensual, seductive. Much like you, by the way. The first night in Rio, after being gone for two weeks, who do you choose to sleep with? Vânia. So I ask: Am I just being crazy?"

"Espinosa, dear, we're not married, we don't live together, we never agreed to be sexually exclusive, I don't even know if I can consider you a boyfriend. There's no question that we're lovers, in the classical and best sense of the word. Our relationship has been going on for years, and I think I can speak for both of us when I say that it's always been very pleasurable. If one of us decides to break it off someday, all we have to do is say the word. We don't have to divide our property, cart off our clothes, or gather up personal items. All it takes is for one of us to say that it's over. If I started wanting to be with a woman, I wouldn't have to go lurking around. So I suggest we enjoy this marvelous Japanese lunch you ordered and the marvelous French wine I brought."

The lunch and the wine lessened the tension. Lessened it—not eliminated it. For the first time, a weekend that should have felt like a reunion felt like they were growing apart. At least verbally. The sex they'd had a few minutes before was as good as ever. Its form, its style might have changed a bit, but not the quality. Espinosa thought about the disassociation between words and bodies, and especially about how long he could stand it. But once the first bottle of wine was finished, he wasn't questioning as much, his thoughts came to him more slowly, and his ideas became muddled. Despite the initial turbulence, the weekend was peaceful, and Espinosa understood that Irene really had missed him.

On Sunday night, Espinosa accompanied Irene to her building in Ipanema, and was on his way back home in a cab when his cell phone rang.

"Espinosa, come back, please."

"What happened?"

"I don't know, but I don't like it at all."

"Is Vânia okay?"

"She's not here. The doorman said she never came back."

A few minutes later, Espinosa rang the bell. He found Irene with her phone book in one hand and her cell phone in the other, pacing up and down the living room.

"The two of us left home together on Saturday morning: I went to your apartment and she went to meet her friends on the beach. She doesn't know Rio that well, but she's street-smart and she knows the names of the beaches in the Zona Sul, besides, obviously, knowing that this beach here is Ipanema, where she'd arranged to meet her friends. We left before noon, and according to the doorman she hadn't come back before eight, when his shift was up. And she still hasn't come back. Two days . . ."

"Could she have gone back to São Paulo? Maybe there was an emergency . . ."

"No. Her things are all still here."

"Do you know the names of the people she was going out with? Do you have any of their phone numbers?"

"Since they were people from here in Rio that she'd met in São Paulo, I didn't bother to write anything down. I know they live in Ipanema, which is why they arranged to meet on Ipanema Beach, right across from the end of my street. I also know that it was a couple and a friend of theirs. I've already called her cell phone, but it's off. There's no sign that she ever came back here."

"Could she have gone on a trip with them to somewhere close by?"

"With nothing more than the clothes on her back? I mean, in a bikini and a beach towel? Without a note or a message on my answering machine? No. Definitely not."

4

After several calls to Rio and São Paulo, Irene managed to track down the couple that Vânia had planned to go out with the day before.

"We didn't see her," the woman said. "We said we'd meet on the sidewalk across from the end of your street, but when we got there Vânia wasn't there. We'd planned to walk down the beach a bit, since she didn't know Ipanema, and then go have lunch, even in our beach clothes, on the terrace of some neighborhood restaurant. Since she wasn't there, we thought that Marcos, our friend, had gotten there earlier and that the two of them had gone off together. Even so, we kept looking for them on the sidewalk and on the beach, in both directions. We called Vânia's cell phone, but it had been turned off. We went to your building and asked the doorman if she was there. He said that she'd left with you. We asked him to check, since she could have come back to get something. He buzzed up, but nobody answered. We went back to the beach and waited where we'd said we'd meet for another hour. She didn't show up. And her phone was off for the rest of the day. Marcos didn't pick up his phone either. And now you're telling me that she didn't come back home or leave any message . . ."

"She didn't say she was going anywhere before meeting you?"

"No. All she said was that if she got there very early she might take a short stroll, just so she wouldn't have to stand still. She also said she'd take a straw hat for the sun. Maybe she and Marcos decided to spend the weekend together . . . by themselves?"

"Without telling us?"

"It might have been some instant passion. Marcos didn't come home either. They've got to be together. What I can tell you to reassure you is that Marcos is one of our oldest friends. He's a very well-known lawyer in Rio; Vânia would be perfectly safe with him. Do you think something else could have happened?"

"I have no idea, but as soon as I find out I'll call you back."

Espinosa, who was listening to the conversation, asked the friend to give him a description of Marcos: age, height, appearance, and so on. From what Irene said, Espinosa understood that Vânia was not only intelligent but canny as well. She'd traveled all over the world and knew how to act in big cities; she wouldn't have gotten lost on a two-block trip to the beach, or walking down a seaside sidewalk.

"On Sunday nights, people tend to be home," Espinosa said. "Try to get in touch with any friends and colleagues Vânia could have talked to about the week she was going to spend in Rio. Ask about any places or people she might have mentioned. Did she do drugs?"

"Not as far as I know," Irene said. "She just likes beer, wine, and spirits, but I've never seen her drunk."

"Tell me more about her. Is she a cold or a passionate person?"

"She's passionate about everything she does, but she can keep her cool in a negotiation, for example."

"Could she fall in love with someone at first sight and agree to do something like a boat trip through Guanabara Bay? Lunch in a picturesque restaurant in Sepetiba or something like that?"

"She could be interested in someone at first sight, but that doesn't mean she'd agree to things that might be dangerous."

"I'm going to the station to make some phone calls and take some measures. If you have any news or remember something, even if it seems insignificant, call me there or on my cell phone."

At the Twelfth Precinct, Espinosa got in touch with the precincts in the Zona Sul, Barra da Tijuca, and the Zona Oeste, giving a description of Vânia and Marcos and asking officers to provide him with any information that might relate to their situation. The police weren't very interested in the disappearances of adults before a certain amount of time had passed, especially a young, attractive woman in the company of a man on a sunny Sunday in Ipanema. But the weekend had ended and she hadn't come home. After alerting the stations, Espinosa called the emergency rooms of the main hospitals. No patient met the description he gave. Finally, he called the military police and gave them the same description of Vânia. It was ten-thirty. He waited another hour for any news. At five minutes to midnight, he went back to Irene's apartment. Vânia had disappeared thirty-six hours ago. Irene was waiting for him in front of the elevator. She was wearing the same clothes she'd had on when Espinosa left her.

"There's nothing involving a woman fitting Vânia's description in any police station. The same goes for emergency rooms. If she'd been involved in any serious accident on the street, she would have been treated by a fire department ambulance and transported to an emergency room in a public hospital. The military police cars are on the lookout for a woman with your friend's characteristics. I left orders for them to call me whenever they have any news, no matter how vague. Now all we can do is wait for communication—from her or from anyone she may be with."

"Are you thinking she was kidnapped?"

"I don't think so. Vânia's not famous, she's not from a rich family, she wasn't driving a car, and the way she was dressed didn't suggest wealth. It also wasn't a quick kidnapping. Too much time has gone by."

"She couldn't have been abducted?"

"How was someone going to abduct a woman like Vânia at high noon in the middle of Ipanema, without anyone seeing anything and without the slightest reaction from her? Only if it was consensual. But I think so much time has gone by. . . . Who would she be cheating on? If she wanted to break it off with someone, all she had to do was go. She didn't need to disappear."

"That certainly didn't happen."

"That what?"

"That . . . the idea of consensual abduction. . . . It sounds like legalese."

"And it is. It's a legal expression. But it doesn't apply to a woman over twenty-one years of age."

"Espinosa, stop being ironic at such a serious moment—"

"I'm not. I'm just answering your question. And you were the one who mentioned abduction, not me. I know that it's a distressing situation and I know you're worried, but what I want to do now is find Vânia, not be ironic . . . if only because I don't like irony; I prefer humor."

"Sorry."

"There's nothing we can do in the next few hours but wait. I gave my cell phone number to my contacts. Why don't you try to sleep a bit while I wait here in the living room in this super-comfortable armchair?"

"I'll wait with you."

"Honey, I'm used to this. I manage to relax and stay alert at the same time. I've done it ever since I entered the police force. I promise that if they call I'll wake you up."

"She could have been kidnapped to . . . to be used sexually."

"I don't think anyone still needs to kidnap a woman to use her sexually, as you say."

"It's not impossible."

"It's not impossible, but it's highly improbable, much less probable than a kidnapping for ransom."

"But even if that happened, couldn't they sexually abuse her?"

"It's not common."

"But can it happen?"

"Irene, the deeper we get into the early-morning hours and the more tired we get, the more terrible our suspicions will become. Let's just hope she's spending a nice weekend with her friend Marcos."

"Fine. I'll try to sleep a bit. Call me . . ."

"I will."

Irene's living room was well appointed, her furniture tastefully chosen, with a wide window looking out at the street; thanks to the central air-conditioning, it was quiet. From where he was sitting, the only view Espinosa had was of the building on the other side of the street. If he felt like going up to the window and twisting his neck, he could, looking toward the beach, make out a diminutive strip of sea at the end of the long corridor of buildings. He preferred the view he had from his apartment in the Peixoto District, of both the square and the hills around it. He'd thought countless times about what it would be like if he and Irene moved in together. Which of their apartments would it be? He wouldn't dream of leaving the charming informality of his apartment in the Peixoto District. But he realized that Irene's apartment was newer and in a better location. And surely more valuable as well. Yet despite the aesthetic refinement of her decoration (or perhaps because of it), Espinosa didn't feel comfortable there. It was too neat, giving the impression that everything was in its natural place and that any alteration in the established order would rupture the balance of a little private cosmos. But just then, sitting in the leather chair with a nice place to rest his feet and nothing more than the weak light of a small lamp breaking the darkness of the living room, he felt restful and quiet. He wasn't even tired. He checked to see if his phone was charged and if the landline, also within arm's reach, was working. He rested his head on the chair, stretched out his legs, and let his mind wander. The first images were of Irene and Vânia on Friday night: their meeting, the trip to the restaurant, the dinner. And two questions: Who is Vânia? Where is she?

Vânia had been mentioned a few times during his weekend conversations with Irene. And based on fragments of those conversations, Espinosa managed to put together an image that roughly answered the question of who she was: thirty-five years old, daughter of German immigrants, born in the hills of southern Brazil, where she'd spent her childhood and adolescence. She'd studied architecture in Porto Alegre, gone to grad school in Buenos Aires and New York, and had done brief periods as an intern and an employee in France and Italy.

She'd met Irene in New York: she was getting her doctorate and Irene was doing a course at MoMA. They met up again in São Paulo and became friends. She worked in a big architecture firm and was professionally respected and financially independent. She'd married a fellow student right after graduation and had gotten divorced less than a year later. Ever since then, she'd had only brief and superficial relationships. She lived by herself in São Paulo.

It wasn't a full picture, but it was enough to have a good idea of her potential.

The night promised to be long and Espinosa was still up. He allowed his subjective impressions to give a bit of depth and color to the portrait Irene had offered. He really didn't think that Vânia was having an affair with Irene (to the extent that "affair" implied a relatively stable relationship), but he also believed in the possibility of sporadic sexual contact between them. They were pretty and seductive women, and he thought that occasionally the two had exercised their charms on each other. He also thought that ingredients like beauty and seductiveness, when played out in the professional realm, made women like them extremely competitive and almost always successful. Espinosa imagined that Vânia was highly intelligent, capable of making daring decisions, as well as someone who didn't pay much attention to normal modes of behavior, though she was probably ethical. He also added the impression that

Vânia was a romantic. He wondered if she was really like that or if that was just what he wanted her to be.

He got up and went to the kitchen to get some water. The air-conditioning dried out his throat and sparked memories of his smoking days. Neither Irene nor Vânia smoked, he thought. Nor did they do drugs. Irene said that Vânia drank moderately and that she was far from being an alcoholic who could lose her bearings and be forcibly taken away by someone. Besides, if she was involved in some police or hospital situation, he would already have been informed, even if she had lost her memory or her consciousness. So all that was left was kidnapping or voluntary departure. He didn't believe the kidnapping scenario applied here. He went into Irene's room and looked at her from the doorway. She stirred in her bed, asleep. Espinosa went back to his chair, rested his head, and closed his eyes, still thinking about Vânia's disappearance. He was half asleep when he heard a noise in the hallway of the apartment. It might have been Irene getting up, or one of the many domestic noises people hardly noticed in their own homes. Then he felt a soft touch on his shoulder. He turned around to take Irene's hand.

"Vânia!"

"Espinosa! What—"

"Vânia, are you okay?" As he asked the question, he looked her up and down, in search of some wound or problem. "What happened to you?"

"Nothing. At least nothing bad. I was on a boat. . . . We just got back tonight—"

"Since yesterday afternoon you've been on a boat . . . at sea?"

"That's right. We almost made it all the way to Angra dos Reis."

"Let's wake up Irene. . . . She'll be so happy to see you . . ."

"Did something happen here? You were sleeping in the living room."

"No. Nothing happened here."

Vânia was still wearing her swimsuit, sandals, and an obviously borrowed man's shirt. They went into the bedroom. Espinosa lightly touched Irene's arm, calling her name, before turning on the lamp on the bedside table.

Irene shot out of bed.

"What happened? Did they find her?" At that instant she saw her friend emerge from behind Espinosa.

"Vânia!" she cried, darting out of bed to hug and kiss her friend.

Irene was crying and laughing simultaneously, and Vânia, still clinging to Irene and holding her up, said the words "boat," "sea," and "Angra," waiting for them alone to explain what had happened.

Espinosa left the two to their embrace, closed the apartment door without making a sound, and went downstairs to look for a taxi.

5

Hugo Breno thought he had it pretty good as an employee of the Caixa Econômica Federal, especially for someone who lived alone, in his own apartment, and in a style he considered almost monastic. The "almost" was because of the hookers he employed to satisfy his biological needs, needs he tried to reduce with his daily exercise routine. He aimed to stay as physically fit as a member of some special military force about to swing into action in enemy territory. Of course, he didn't train in the jungle or jump out of planes with a parachute; his theater of operations was exclusively urban. His hours at the Caixa Econômica made his exercise easier. He could use the early-morning and evening hours. Every morning, no matter what the weather, he ran up and down the whole length of Copacabana Beach, on the sand, and then swam two hundred meters, no matter what the conditions in the sea. At home, he did his sit-ups and push-ups and worked out his biceps on the bar he'd installed in the doorway of his bedroom. He didn't smoke or drink. He could stand long periods of privation. Yet he'd never had to test his physical preparedness in conditions that exceeded his daily life. From ten to five he was a bank employee. He efficiently executed his duties, he never missed work or arrived late, he hardly spoke to his colleagues, and he never got upset when clients complained. The worst threat was boredom. But he thought that was made up for by the parallel reality that awaited him after his shift, until ten the next morning.

The idea to sign up for the test for placement in the Caixa Econômica occurred to him when he found out that Espinosa had secured his job with the police through an open test. Their motives were probably different. Espinosa was motivated by the desire to get married, so he was looking for a government job that could guarantee him financial security, without a boss who could fire him on a whim. Breno's boss was anonymous and impersonal and they didn't even have to meet. As for getting married, he wasn't planning on it. It wasn't even a vague possibility. He regretted terribly that Espinosa had done so, an error it had taken him ten years to realize. Hugo Breno wondered for what purpose people tried to make life more complicated. Women complicate men's lives, just as men surely complicate women's lives. So whose idea was marriage, anyway? Wasn't it enough to screw and then move on? What did marriage add to the sex? Surely it didn't add anything—it only subtracted. And the first thing marriage took away was happiness. Espinosa was proof of this: a sad man, aged by his memory, tired. A few more years and he wouldn't be able to go up the two flights of stairs without getting to his door out of breath, his heart thumping in his chest. Now, after another decade had gone by, Espinosa was trying to take up the old path, as if that were possible. Once he'd chosen one of the two paths (which was not only physical but temporal), it was impossible to return and take the other. Once you'd been married, there was no way you could stop being that way. At most, someone could become unmarried. Which only added an "un" to the word "married," which meant kids, memories, guilt, resentments . . .

It was true that Espinosa kept his old classiness and dignity. It was like something he'd been born with, a personal trait that experience had added to. For that reason, despite the error of his marriage and his new attempt with his girlfriend, Hugo still saw Espinosa as a model. Even though the model had been strained a bit, though its best days were past, it was still a model. He hadn't stopped admiring him simply because he had changed. Their age difference, though slight, made Espinosa the model he had looked up to since he was a boy. Espinosa was still his older brother.

Hugo didn't like weekends. It wasn't that he couldn't stand them—he even thought they had certain advantages over other days of the week (not having to work being one of them), but there was something about them that bothered him. Sundays more than Saturdays. Saturdays weren't as bad; they were like a weekday where you didn't have to go to work. At least for him. Sundays, though, felt like false or failed days, in which everything was available but nothing was possible. The closed shops cleared out the streets. The day felt abandoned. Everything felt artificial, including rest.

On Sundays, he went for his run down the Avenida Atlântica as soon as the sun came up. It was exactly enough time before the beachgoers started arriving and taking up all the room. It was impossible to run on the sidewalk after eight. Swimming wasn't a problem. Most bathers didn't venture beyond the surf, and he liked to swim past the breaking waves, parallel to the beach.

He'd just run and swum and was on his way back home. He didn't feel any attraction to the compact mass of people that occupied the entire strip of sand on the beach, forming a stationary agglomerate of languid, nearly naked, sweating people with sand stuck to their bodies. He thought it was repellent. It wasn't the same kind of crowd that was permanently moving down the sidewalks, dressed, clean. From the beach to his building, going up Siqueira Campos, was a straight line. He could also go down Figueiredo Magalhães, one block over, and pass through the Peixoto District to check out Espinosa's building. Afterward all he had to do was take the little side street back to Siqueira Campos. He didn't expect to see Espinosa waving from the window. He wasn't the pope. But it was enough for Hugo to see the open window, a sign that he was home, probably reading the papers, as he did on weekends.

It was both confirmation and compensation. The window was open; Espinosa was home. He couldn't see if he was reading the papers. Wherever he went in the square, all he could see was a little part of the living room, the wall with heaps of books on it, the top of a standing lamp, a few pictures or photographs, and a lighting fixture on the ceiling that looked like it was made of smoked glass (another thing they had in common: he also had a light fixture like that). But that morning, after spending a few minutes observing the two windows of the living room, he saw, besides Espinosa's head . . . Irene's, his girlfriend's. It wasn't so usual for her to spend Saturday night there too. It must have been a special weekend.

Espinosa had gone to bed late the night before and got up early on Monday morning. Even though Vânia's disappearance had turned out fine, he suspected that the consequences of that weekend wouldn't be so positive. At least for him. He called off the alert he'd put through to the other precincts and the military police and concentrated on the investigation of Dona Laureta's death.

The only thing that prevented him from considering it an accident was the visit she had paid to the station with the clear intent of speaking with the chief. Not with him, Espinosa. She didn't know him. She wanted to talk to whoever the chief was. Nobody would make such a specific request just to say that her cat was missing. It wasn't a threat to the cat that the lady didn't even possess, but to herself. The fact that she preferred to come back later instead of speaking just then to Detective Welber showed that there was no urgency to what she had to communicate. In a word, it was an important enough matter that she could discuss it only with the boss, but not urgent, having to do with an immediate threat. Another point that in Espinosa's opinion ruled out an accident was the fact that several people said she seemed to have been pushed from the curb into the street, though nobody there had witnessed the supposed push. It occurred to Espinosa that she might have stumbled or tripped. Which would make it neither a murder nor a suicide. An accident. But that hypothesis wasn't very plausible. The sidewalk wasn't wet, and nobody around had seen anything that might have made her slip. Besides, when people slip they usually fall into a sitting position and aren't propelled forward. But though the hypothesis was implausible, it wasn't less probable than the idea that she had been pushed under the wheels of the bus.

It was four in the afternoon on a hot and bureaucratic day, the kind of day that inspired Espinosa to fantasize about jumping ship. He was dreaming about creating the post of administrative chief, leaving the nonadministrative chief (he'd have to invent a name for him) just one police duty: thinking. Of course, he wouldn't be a speculative thinker, a kind of police Platonist, but committed to an essentially investigative kind of thinking oriented toward solving crimes and capturing criminals. The policeman-philosopher's dream was interrupted by the arrival of Welber, and by the way he arrived, tapping his finger on the glass divider, Espinosa knew that he had good news.

"Chief, I've just gotten back from the NIED."

Espinosa wrinkled his brow and made a questioning gesture with his hands.

"The National Institute for the Education of the Deaf," Welber said. "I took them the video of Dona Laureta's conversation with the cashier. All they could do was read their lips during fragments of the initial conversation, but they agreed that the conversation involved much more than what the cashier told us. Part of the dialogue is impossible to read because of the security bars and their position, but it's clear enough that the conversation lasted much longer than the initial exchange. The two really did talk a lot more than the cashier said."

"Have you already asked him about this?"

"Not yet. I want to look at the tapes from earlier months to see if I can find anything else. It's a tiring and monotonous task. It's the same scene, without sound, repeated hundreds of times. The picture is bad quality, out of focus, and the movement of people seems not to be continuous. That almost makes it impossible to do more with lip-reading."

"What did you find out about this cashier?"

"His name is Hugo Breno, he's a good worker, he

doesn't miss work, he doesn't get in late, he's never had problems with customers or colleagues. Nobody knows much about his private life, except that he's single and has lived at the same address for more than thirty years."

"What's the address?"

"On Siqueira Campos, near the subway station, a few blocks from the bank where he works."

"And close to where Dona Laureta lived," Espinosa added.

"And also close to where you live."

"Close to the station."

"Pure coincidence," said Welber with a smile.

"Death in the neighborhood," said Espinosa without a smile. "Tomorrow morning I want to stop by the Caixa Econômica. I want to see what kind of a man this is."

It was the first day of autumn. Not that, in Rio de Janeiro, that meant an expressive or immediate change of climate, but in homage to the calendar, the weather had in fact shifted a bit overnight. The day began gray, rainy, and the temperature had fallen a few degrees, enough to allow Espinosa to walk to the branch of the Caixa Econômica, a kilometer away, without breaking a sweat. He thought it was strange that everyone involved in the case lived within a circle a kilometer in diameter, whose center was the Twelfth Precinct. Even Welber, who was investigating the case and who had always lived in Tijuca, had just moved to Copacabana, within the circumscribed area. That coincidence was not, for Espinosa, a sign of any real mystery, but just something that made him aware of possible relationships between all those people. The chief didn't much believe in coincidences, especially when they resulted in deaths.

It was ten-fifteen when he went into the bank. Even from far away, he easily spotted Hugo Breno in one of the windows. Welber's description had been precise. He took a number as soon as he got in and looked for a chair at a comfortable distance from the teller, where he could observe him like anybody else sitting there. There were few seats available, all quite far from the counter. With his ticket in hand, Espinosa kept looking for a spot while he watched the numbers on the screen and observed Hugo Breno through the window. He didn't look unfamiliar; he had the idea that he knew him, though he didn't know from where. Even the name Hugo Breno wasn't unfamiliar.

The cashier had just finished helping a customer and had already pressed the button for the next number when he saw Espinosa move toward a chair that had opened up. The impact was just like the one he had felt when he was eleven, when he saw Espinosa for the first time. Back then, the square in the Peixoto District hadn't been fixed up. Neither the heavy fountain, the fences, nor all the prefabricated playground equipment had

arrived. In those days games didn't require the interven-
tion of child development professionals and the square
was a generous open space. The wooden benches were
the most comfortable and welcome acquisition. The
earthen field where the neighborhood kids played soccer had been preserved. It was in the middle of a game,
during the summer holidays, that he'd seen for the first
time the boy the others called Espinosa. He thought it
was a nickname, since he'd never known anyone with
a name like that. Espinosa was only a little older than
Hugo, but he seemed much bigger, stronger, and better
looking. He had a well-made body, defined muscles in
his legs and arms, though he wasn't very old, and he
moved his body with elegance, besides being a talented soccer player. He didn't talk much. He wasn't
everyone's friend, though everyone tried to be friends
with him. He didn't do anything just to seem friendly,
though he was naturally amiable.

From then on, Espinosa became Hugo's idol. He did
everything to be where Espinosa was. He tried to participate in the same games, whether on his team or the
opposing one. He tried to find out where he lived, if he
had brothers or sisters, where he went to school, everything about him. But there was one thing he wanted
more than anything else. That was to belong to Espinosa's
group, who rode their bikes through the neighborhood,
up and down the streets, which Hugo wasn't allowed to
do because of his age. Hugo was too small to participate

in such daring adventures. He remembered perfectly the English bicycle with which Espinosa led his small group of biking friends. Maybe "led" wasn't the right word. Espinosa was just a member of the group without having been appointed leader, but there was no question that his English bicycle and the way he interacted with his friends made him the group's most important figure. And it was he himself, Espinosa, who at that moment had just come into the waiting room at the Caixa Econômica. Hugo Breno noted that Espinosa was looking for somewhere to sit. There was a seat available at the very front, facing the window, but he chose one farther away. He was absolutely sure that the chief was there for him. First his two assistants had come, and now he was here in the flesh. He was wondering whether the chief would come up to him or if he should take the initiative to meet him first.

Espinosa noticed the cashier observing him and felt a bit uncomfortable. Hugo didn't watch him openly but discreetly kept an eye on him, as he was doing with Hugo. He thought that the cashier might know that he was the chief of the precinct in the neighborhood. Espinosa was more or less well known. His picture had come out in the papers and he'd been interviewed on television, so it was natural that people should look at him. But no, that wasn't it. He felt observed in the same way that he was observing the man. Even more so. With every passing moment, he became more and more sure that he knew him. Not at random, from having seen him on the street, but from something he couldn't quite remember.

While he mechanically helped the elderly gentleman who was presenting two or three cards in order to withdraw his benefits, Hugo Breno followed Espinosa's every glance, every movement, trying to guess what he was thinking. At a certain moment, he had the impression that the chief was going to get up. It could be to come up to the window or to leave. And he felt that he couldn't miss the opportunity that would be the only time Espinosa would come looking for him and not vice versa, in his own timid attempts. He thought about closing the window, in a clear sign that he was available to talk. As soon as he finished dealing with the old man, he turned off the light on his counter and looked for Espinosa, but he had just risen from his seat and was walking away without a backward glance.

6

It was Tuesday at noon. Espinosa and Irene still hadn't spoken since Vânia's reappearance on Sunday night. The receptionist put the call through to the chief's office.

"Espinosa, what's going on?"

"Well, just since yesterday, here in the neighborhood, a teenager stabbed his grandmother to death, a man was found dead inside the trunk of a car, an assailant dropped his gun while holding up a senior citizen, a passerby grabbed the gun and fired two shots into the assailant—"

"Fuck! I don't mean that kind of goings-on."

"You called a police station to ask what's going on."

"Espinosa, I'll talk to you later on tonight. I feel like now isn't even the right time to say hello."

"Which, now that you mention it, you didn't say."

"Hello. And good-bye," she said, hanging up.

After less than a minute, she called back.

"Sorry, I was rude."

"It's fine. I wasn't that welcoming either."

"Can we have lunch? Maybe in that trattoria you like."

Suggesting the trattoria was an obvious olive branch. Less tradition-bound, Irene always preferred the restaurants in Ipanema to those in Copacabana, so Espinosa was happy to accept the gesture. He left immediately and managed to reach the Italian restaurant in time to get a table next to the window. Not for the view—the windows were curtained—but because those were the most private tables. Before Irene got there, all the others filled up. The usual customers were businesspeople, bankers, professionals, and local residents who preferred to eat out. The food was typical of an Italian trattoria, and the regular presence of the boss guaranteed quality service.

Irene arrived dressed with an elegant simplicity, but even so the whole restaurant noticed her. Espinosa got up to greet her and help her with the files and the purse she held in her hands.

"I'm going straight to work from here," she said, smiling as if to apologize.

They looked at each other, holding hands on top of the table, clearly happy to be in the other's company, despite the phone call a half hour before.

"So, babe, who were you annoyed with? Me or my friend?"

"I wasn't annoyed with you. I just didn't call yesterday. As for Vânia, I didn't like what she did."

"You didn't like that she went sailing?"

"She didn't go sailing. She left on Saturday at noon and came back at midnight on Sunday without saying a word, without leaving a note with the doorman, without a phone call. I don't believe that, on a supposed boat that could go from Rio to Angra and return in that same amount of time, there was not a single cell phone, or that the boat itself didn't have any means of communication. Not having told us anything was a way of worrying us and punishing us for spending the weekend together, without her. She decided to punish you for not staying with her; and me too, for being responsible for your not staying with her; and both of us, ruining our weekend. It's not only vengeful, it's irresponsible. Today it's Tuesday. She came to spend a week. We'll see what she gets up to before Saturday or Sunday. As for the sailing, it doesn't matter in the least whether it really happened."

"You really think that's what it was?"

"I do. But I don't hate her for it. The problem is just that she caught me unawares."

Irene didn't try to defend her friend. Even if only because she thought that Espinosa's theory could be right.

"Fine," she said. "Let's eat."

They didn't order wine since both had to work that afternoon, but they did have the codfish risotto.

Espinosa put Irene into a taxi and walked back to the station, going up the Rua Hilário de Gouveia. Three themes kept bouncing around his head: Irene and Vânia, Dona Laureta, Hugo Breno. The day had begun with his unannounced visit to the Caixa Econômica branch, and at the window was the man who had talked to the retiree on the day she died, a conversation that had gone on longer than he had described to Welber and Ramiro. The man's features reminded Espinosa of someone he knew was close to him, familiar, though strangely enough he couldn't identify him. The name Hugo Breno also rang a bell. He tried to recall some former colleague, someone who might have started with him on the police force and then decided to work at a bank instead; he tried to remember his colleagues from the time he worked at the First Precinct, in the Praça Mauá, but he realized that he was on the wrong track—that vague memory didn't have anything to do with the police. Then he started thinking about fellow students in college, but there again he didn't remember anyone who fit the description. Hugo Breno lived on the Rua Siqueira Campos, close to the Peixoto District, so the two of them might have crossed paths countless times without leaving a clear impression in his memory. He might have been some unknown neighbor. Nothing more than that. Espinosa kept walking; he was almost at the station. The fact that they lived so close also suggested, for some odd reason, that he was getting closer to the man. He kept walking. He walked by the door to the station without pausing and without going in, his eyes cast down to the sidewalk, like a dog who has lost his owner. Two detectives who were chatting on the sidewalk greeted him and watched as he kept walking up the street, as if the station had moved to a different block. But they knew the chief well enough not to be surprised by his eccentricities.

Espinosa walked in no particular direction, though he noticed, after he crossed Siqueira Campos, that he was being drawn toward the Peixoto District. Minutes later, he crossed the square on his way to his building. But instead of going all the way there, he stopped in the middle of the square and started walking in circles across the grass. He immediately remembered the dust thrown up by the soccer games of his childhood and the cries of the little players; he saw himself sweeping the earth with a tree branch to get the ground ready for a game of marbles, remembering also the discussions about whether this was going to be a real game or just for fun. His memories emerged spontaneously, without any effort, and among the many faces of his childhood friends one grew sharper and sharper. It wasn't a visage that quickly came to mind; rather, an image came to mind, but not so much the individual faces within it. His own group of friends appeared like a group of bodies without defined physiognomies. And he didn't know if it was the past that was coming up through that image or if his current imagination was filling in the gaps in his memory, giving every member of that group an identity. One of the first faces to turn up was a boy's . . . and it was his . . . Hugo Breno, the man from the Caixa. Not the image of him now, but of a boy like him. The cashier as a boy. He had a body and a face, but not a name. Despite that, Espinosa had no doubt. He remembered that the boy was a little younger than he was, maybe a year or two. He was also the smallest one. That's why they called him Little Hugo. He wasn't very close to Espinosa, they weren't friends, but they saw each other often. It made sense. If Hugo had been living in the building on Siqueira Campos since he was a boy, he would have been ten or eleven at the time. More than thirty years before, an eleven-year-old boy could perfectly well have gone by himself to the Peixoto District, only two blocks away, to play in the square. That was why Espinosa had that particular impression of familiarity but not intimacy. Since he was younger, the boy belonged to the younger group, even though for certain games they might get together. But there was something else that had to do not so much with the image of the boy but with the feeling he got from the image of the boy. A feeling of strangeness. The vague idea that something had happened to that boy or to someone connected to him. Espinosa didn't remember (or didn't know) what it was, but something strange was connected to the memory. He tried to force himself to think, but the memory got more and more hazy. He kept walking slowly around the square for another fifteen minutes; then he finally headed back to the station. The rest of the afternoon was dedicated to childhood memories, trying to clear out the more recent ones, which covered up the older ones. It didn't work. At least not that afternoon.

Once he'd finished his shift, dealing with retirees and pensioners, and had done all he had to do in-house, Hugo Breno left the branch of the Caixa Econômica, still disappointed with Chief Espinosa's hurried exit. It was a little past five and the movement of people along the sidewalks of the Rua Barata Ribeiro was nothing more than average. Instead of going straight home, he headed toward the Avenida Copacabana, where there were lots more people, though the thoroughfare still hadn't reached the level of saturation it would attain at six. He crossed the Avenida Copacabana and kept walking toward the beach.

He didn't have any interest in seeing the ocean or appreciating the sunset. For him, the oft-praised beauty of Copacabana Beach would do nothing to put him in a better mood. Nature proved useless when dealing with human problems and feelings. Whether beautiful or not, it was useless either way. The only place man can feel good, he thought, is among humans. The only thing that resembles man is man himself. Man does not resemble nature. Among the crowd, the human individual can either lose himself in the homogenous mass or maintain his individuality. The feeling of belonging to something yet still keeping one's difference is one of the supreme experiences of man among the crowd. In nature, whether the surroundings are beautiful or ugly, pleasant or unpleasant, man will always be different. Always a figure, never in the background. A tree in the forest gets lost and diluted in the forest, becoming a part of the undifferentiated background; a man in the middle of the forest will never be background but always be his own character, an irreducible and aberrant difference. That's why nature didn't interest Hugo. When dealing with human matters, human sentiments and fears, nature was irrelevant. That's what he was thinking while he was walking, killing time until he got back to the Avenida Copacabana. Once he got there, he let himself get lost in the crowd for more than an hour. Once he'd done that, he could separate himself out from them, refreshed, and head home.

It was dark when he opened the door to his apartment. No surprises. There was nobody waiting for him, just as there was nothing different from when he'd left that morning. Nobody had come into the apartment in his absence. He couldn't stand the thought of anyone having the freedom to go through every room, every wardrobe, every drawer, while he was out working. Not that there was anything special to be ransacked; there were no hidden secrets, no stashed-away valuables. And it was precisely for that reason that he would have felt invaded. Not because of what was hidden, but because everything was on display. It was the nudity of his life that would be exposed. That's why he didn't want a maid. He wouldn't even allow an occasional cleaning lady. He himself cleaned the apartment. He had a washer and a dryer. He himself ironed his shirts and pants. With the exception of vegetables, everything he ate he bought frozen. In a word, he considered himself autonomous, independent, and almost wholly self-sufficient. Physical contact with others, men or women, made him uncomfortable. When something went wrong with his body, he had recourse to health professionals. Friends were unnecessary.

As soon as he came in, he opened the windows in the front and the back of the apartment, as he always did, took off his clothes, put on some shorts, and started doing his series of abdominal exercises, push-ups, and bar exercises. He didn't need musical accompaniment. Nothing to remind him of a gym. After a shower he went to the nearest supermarket to buy his dinner.

After the meeting with his team at the end of the day, Espinosa called Welber and Ramiro into his office.

"Any news?" he asked the two of them.

"We think we've got something, boss, though it might make the case even more complicated than it already is," Ramiro said.

As an inspector, it was Ramiro's job to lay out what he and Detective Welber had found. Espinosa trusted them and they almost always worked together.

"Well, Welber confirmed with the National Institute

for the Education of the Deaf that the cashier and the old lady talked much longer than what he had told us. That's the first thing, and that's not news to you. The second thing is that it wasn't the first time they'd talked. They talked at least once a month for the last three months, as far back as the tapes go. And every time the conversation was just as extensive, or more extensive than what's necessary to hand over some money at the counter."

"And did you, Ramiro, get anything else?"

"I did. And this is news . . . as well as strange. Looking at Dona Laureta's old address books, I found the number of a lady whose address is the same as Hugo Breno's. At some date I didn't manage to nail down, the phone and the address were scratched out, as if the person had moved . . . or died. In other words, Dona Laureta and Hugo Breno's mother knew each other and spoke, at least on the phone. Of course, that might not have anything to do with our story. They lived nearby, they met at the market, they were more or less the same age, both widows, became friends, and . . ."

"And?"

"Well, that's it, Chief—it's difficult to infer anything about Dona Laureta's possible murder from the simple fact that the two of them were friends," Ramiro concluded.

"We'll see," Espinosa said. "Two widowed neighbor ladies become friends. One of them has a son who's around forty who lives with her and works at the Caixa

Econômica. The other doesn't have children and lives alone. The one with the son dies. A year later, the friend dies in suspicious circumstances, after a tense conversation with her dead friend's son, who is a cashier at the agency where she picks up her pension every month. You know that I don't place much store in coincidences. And here there are too many coincidences. Of course, we have an explanation for that: they're not coincidences. If the cashier's mother was a friend of the lady's, her son should know her. When, after the mother's death, he discovers that her friend gets her pension at the same branch where he's a teller, it's only natural that they would exchange a few words. So there's nothing strange about those facts. But then it so happens that she dies hours after talking to him and minutes after coming to the station to talk to the chief. Something's not right here. Or missing. Find out what."

That night, at home, after washing the plate and silverware from a meal whose exact contents he could no longer precisely describe, Espinosa gazed out at the square from the little balcony outside his French windows. Ever since he was ten years old, when he moved to that apartment with his parents, whenever he was mulling over some problem (except for mathematics) he stepped onto that balcony and let his eyes wander through the movement in the square or onto the green of the hill in the distance. One of the differences now was the position of his body. When he was ten, he could rest his chin on an arm sitting atop the cast-iron balcony, and now his entire torso stuck out above the railing. The landscape had changed as well. The square had lost the bamboo grove akin to its original state and had acquired a few urban improvements. But the biggest change had been in the spirit of the neighborhood, which, like the city itself, had suffered a reverse metamorphosis: instead of transforming from a caterpillar into a butter-fly, it had gone from a butterfly to a caterpillar.

The current population of the city, and to a lesser extent of the neighborhood, lived under a curfew deter-mined by the drug traffickers. Even the peaceful area around the Peixoto District was not free of the effects of its proximity to the Ladeira dos Tabajaras, where internal disputes for the control of the traffic some-times burst the borders of the favela and spilled into the square and the neighborhood. That scenario, remote but not entirely unthinkable, was not easy for a police chief to contemplate, especially when he was trying to superimpose two moments from his personal history onto two moments in the history of his neighborhood. He didn't know if the neighborhood and the city would recover, someday, a bit of its lost peace.

But the neighborhood and the square were still rec-ognizable to the adult Espinosa. The difficulty he was having was recognizing in Hugo Breno the boy who'd played soccer in the square. Espinosa forced his visual memory far beyond the present he had in front of his eyes and tried to visualize the boy, a little smaller than he was, struggling against his shyness and trying to make himself known and get invited to participate in the games. He remembered the boy being accepted. He remembered that even though he was little he tried his very best to do as well or better than the older boys. He also remembered that something had happened to that boy. Something bad.

The phone must have been ringing for a while when Espinosa snapped out of his daydreams.

"Espinosa, are you busy?"

"No . . ."

"It's Vânia. Sorry for calling you so late."

"What do you mean, so late? It's only eight-thirty."

"I thought you might be resting."

"I was trying to remember something that happened in my childhood."

"And did you?"

"Only partially. It's something important, one of those things that you don't forget but that time distorts."

"Something bad?"

"I still don't know."

"How do you mean?"

"I've forgotten the most important part."

"Ah."

"Can I help you with something?" Espinosa asked.

"You must think that what I did this weekend was stupid."

"Not stupid. Cunning."

"Cunning?"

"Yes. Cunning."

"Espinosa, you really are an interesting guy."

"Is that a compliment?"

"It depends on what you mean by 'cunning.'"

"Shrewd."

"That doesn't help much."

"Wily, tricky, catty, crafty, deceitful . . ."

"Ah . . ."

"Do you think that's good or bad?"

"It can be either, depending on what you mean by them," Vânia said.

"I think they're attractive," Espinosa replied.

"Those adjectives?"

"When applied to a woman like you."

"And would you like to see if they really do apply to me?"

"I'd love to."

"Today?"

"Now."

Espinosa could hardly believe it when, a half hour later, Vânia rang the bell and came up the stairs with the same energy Irene had several years before. That mood, however, gave way to an almost modest carefulness when she embraced him upon entering the apartment, a carefulness Espinosa noted when he felt the partial touch of their bodies, at least in the first moments of their meeting. And he also noticed that his own body was tense, all tense, but especially his legs. Slowly, however, they relaxed, until their bodies grasped each other entirely.

Up to that point, neither had said a word. Only when they gestured to take off their clothes did Vânia look around, as if to find the way to the bedroom. That was when she started to undress, and even then she didn't do so until she'd seen Espinosa unbutton and remove his shirt.

She gave herself over to him slowly. First she allowed her body to be explored by Espinosa's lips and hands, an exploration that began with her hair, continued along her face and neck, then went down her whole body all the way to her feet, without neglecting a single part in between. Only then did she start to explore Espinosa's body, an activity that for him felt deliciously interminable. Vânia's nudity was stunningly beautiful, but Espinosa thought that despite the freedom he felt caressing her, he ought to be careful, because the equilibrium of the moment was much more unstable than it would be if he waited for Vânia to take the lead.

"Are you sorry you came?" he asked.

"Of course not."

"Worried about something? Irene maybe . . ."

"No. Irene has nothing to do with the fact that we're here."

"Then forget the question."

"I already have."

But she hadn't. Espinosa clearly felt the division between wanting to hand herself over and needing to resist, both of which were intense. The intriguing and ambivalent experience that he was having was like being in bed with a Nordic goddess who would let him stroke her anywhere but whose body language made him think it would be a mistake to go further. And all he wanted just then was to go further, before he went crazy. He didn't go crazy, but he couldn't go further. When he could no longer contain himself and Vânia noticed that she was starting to be penetrated, she moved Espinosa's body away and got up with a start. As she was apologizing, she began putting on her clothes. In a few seconds she left, repeating under her breath: "Sorry, sorry, sorry . . ."

A half hour after Vânia's sudden retreat, and with the sound of the slamming door still ringing in his ears, and with every inch of Vânia's body still present in his senses, and without understanding what had happened in that bed, and feeling naked and ridiculous, pissed off, Espinosa took a cold shower, which he hated doing.

He got dressed and went outside.

Nothing to do then. There was no immediate substitute for a woman like Vânia. And even if there was, it wouldn't have been right, either for him or for the substitute. He wasn't one to drink to drown out his romantic frustrations. Or one to stuff himself with food. There was no question of reading, writing, or working. Walking down the Avenida Atlântica obviously wouldn't solve the problem, but it would help him to alleviate the tension. On the walk, he would try to decipher the enigma.

The enigma was that a pretty, intelligent, experienced woman would call a man asking if he wanted to go to bed with her and then, once she was in that man's arms, would suddenly turn into a teenager about to be deflowered by her boyfriend. Compared to Irene's exuberant sexuality, Vânia's sexual behavior had been almost meek, frightened, which hardly squared with the image she presented. The most paradoxical thing was the distance between her proposition and the actual event, between the "Would you like to see . . . ?" and the "Sorry, sorry, sorry," between the telephone seduction and the hysterical retreat. Vânia was no virgin. But at least that night, she had been floored by a fear verging on panic when about to consummate the act. That was the enigma: Isn't that what she had wanted to happen? Wasn't that the explicit proposition she herself had made? No matter how long he walked, Espinosa couldn't figure out what had happened in that bed . . . in the last moments. Maybe she herself couldn't have explained it. Or, even worse, maybe there wasn't any enigma at all, and he was trying to come up with a hidden meaning for something that was nothing more than what it appeared. Vânia regretted the proposition she'd made over the phone. When a game of seduction turned into a concrete fact, she beat a retreat. But Espinosa was convinced that the truth was much more complex than that simplistic explanation. The incontestable fact was that he'd never gotten so close to the pleasure of the gods without having to die for it.

He kept walking, indifferent to the sea, the weather, the people he was passing, and, after a while, he became indifferent even to his own thoughts. He'd walked down the entire length of Copacabana Beach. Tired, he went home.

Ever since Welber and Selma had moved from Tijuca to Copacabana to live in a rented apartment on the Rua Santa Clara, the couple's life had undergone a radical transformation. They were now steps from the beach, they had all the shopping of Copacabana at their doorstep, and their cultural life had been enriched. This, despite the financial strains resulting from the more expensive rent and the urban noise that they weren't used to. But what made the detective the happiest was being able to walk to the station in ten minutes, a trip that formerly had taken him more than an hour and required two different modes of transportation.

By Wednesday morning, nine days after Dona Laureta's death, Welber and Ramiro had gathered evidence not only of a connection between Hugo Breno and Dona Laureta but also suggestions that the woman and his mother had been friends for years. Even considering these materially inconsistent signs, the two thought that they could be taken as meaning that the three people—two of which were dead—had something in common, something more than simply being neighbors. What didn't make sense was how the link between the two ladies and the son of one of them could have produced a murder.

The two policemen were waiting for the boss to finish a call that was obviously boring him and to which he was only contributing with a few monosyllabic responses, which later evolved into unintelligible grunts. Finally, the conversation ended. Which was to say that the other person must have said good-bye, because the chief simply replaced the phone.

Ramiro explained to the chief what they'd found about the connections between the pensioner, the lady, and her son.

"Then examine Hugo Breno's working life from the day he started working at the Caixa Econômica. Take note of any irregularities and see if there's any sign of mental disturbance since he's been working there."

"We already did, boss. Not investigating mental disturbances, but his behavior in general. He's a model worker. He never misses a day, he doesn't get there late, he doesn't take sick days, he doesn't cause trouble with anyone, and his performance is considered excellent. The only problem, which isn't exactly a problem, is that he doesn't make friends with anyone, even though he is very polite when people speak to him."

"The other thing I want is for you to follow Hugo Breno from the moment he leaves his job in the afternoon until he goes to sleep. The same thing in the morning, until he goes to work. One at a time, on alternating days. If you find it's too tiring, we can call in someone else to share the work. For now it's just the two of you. I want to know if he meets up with anyone, if he goes anywhere, if he's a member of any religious organization, what he does for recreation or sport. He has to hang out with someone—friends, girlfriends, boyfriends, guru, whatever. Be careful not to be seen: he already knows us and knows we're keeping an eye on him."

"We'll need a bicycle," Ramiro said.

"A bicycle?"

"For the mornings. He leaves home at sunrise. He runs up and down Copacabana Beach, and then swims around two hundred meters. And then he runs back home. We're not in that kind of shape, chief."

"Fine. Rent a bicycle. There's a store a block away."

Espinosa's effort to remember the event in his childhood connected to Hugo Breno was getting mixed up with his memories of the day before with Vânia. The more he thought about the former, the more the latter took over in his mind. He stopped thinking about it. In the middle of the afternoon, the image of Vânia leaving the bedroom naked gave way to Vânia as a little girl, dead. Of course, it couldn't be a memory of Vânia. It wasn't Vânia who had collapsed and died. Why was she a girl, and why was she dead? Who was that girl? She had fallen in a building. A dead girl inside a building. Not inside an apartment; maybe in a hallway or a stairwell. In the Peixoto District. He himself was a boy too.

He started rummaging through his head and figured out a rough date. Welber hadn't yet gone out to follow Hugo Breno and promptly answered his call.

"Welber, I want you to go through the Rio papers looking for news about the death of a girl about eleven years old, in the Peixoto District. It must have been around 1975. I don't know the exact date. I don't know the girl's name. I just know that she must have been around eleven and that she must have been murdered. We can find something in the newspaper archives. Try the most important ones and the ones that cover crime news. It's no use looking on the Internet because the papers have only been digitized up to about twenty years back. I think that you can look in the papers themselves, in the National Library. You can delegate the job to someone you think is good at that kind of thing."

"Girl, eleven, found dead, suspected murder, Peixoto District, 1975," Welber noted as Espinosa repeated the facts. "We have a new detective, Chaves, who's good at research."

Welber assigned the task to Chaves, emphasizing that it was a special request made by Chief Espinosa. He went to his locker, took some gear from inside a box, changed his pants and shirt, and went down to the first floor of the station. Then he went to wait for Hugo Breno at the branch of the Caixa Econômica.

At five in the afternoon, the guard opened the staff

door and Hugo Breno came out. Stopping on the sidewalk, he looked both ways, walked to the corner, waited
for the light to change, and crossed the street in the
direction of the Avenida Copacabana. He walked unhurriedly, but without seeming to be just out for a stroll.
His gaze seemed to take in what was going on around
him, as if he was looking for something in particular.
Nothing in him was spontaneous, but it all seemed natural. Welber walked ten meters behind him, sure that
he couldn't be recognized. Not even Espinosa would
recognize him in this getup if he walked by him in the
street.

When Hugo Breno got to the Avenida Copacabana,
he looked to both sides as if evaluating the situation,
and once again waited for the light, crossed the avenue,
and kept walking toward the beach. On the Avenida
Atlântica, he stayed close to the buildings and kept
walking. He didn't look at the sea or at the scenery, and
he didn't seem interested by the people either. He
seemed to have a defined goal that he was heading
toward relentlessly. After walking for almost a half
hour down the Avenida Atlântica, he went back to the
Avenida Copacabana, checked out both sidewalks for a
few seconds, chose the one that seemed to Welber to be
the busiest, and entered the flow of pedestrians. His
pace suffered a drastic reduction, but he didn't seem to
mind; to the contrary, he seemed quite peaceful. He
walked for more than an hour, in both directions down

the avenue, Welber tailing him, eventually heading back to the corner of Siqueira Campos and up the street to the building where he lived. During the whole journey, from the moment he walked out of the bank until he entered his building, Hugo Breno didn't stop in a single shop, didn't pause to look at anything in particular, and didn't speak to anyone. When, two hours later, the light in his apartment went out, Welber waited for another half hour and then went home.

That same afternoon, Ramiro managed to speak to one of Dona Laureta's two remaining friends. She no longer lived at the address listed in Dona Laureta's phone book, and it was only possible to find her thanks to another friend, a remainder of the old group of widows, who indicated an old hotel in the neighborhood of Flamengo as the last address she had for her. She couldn't say if she was still alive.

Ramiro discovered that she was alive and that she would be pleased to meet him. The conversation was productive.

Espinosa wanted to get a call from Vânia explaining what happened the night before. Though it wasn't exactly an explanation he wanted. He just wanted the presence of Vânia, which in and of itself would explain things, without explanatory speeches. Not for them to take up where they left off—though he did desire that, ardently—but he just wanted to get rid of the feeling of rejection that had been planted in his mind. Vânia's gesture of pushing away his body and rushing from the scene left the strong impression that something in him had caused that rejection.

The worst thing was that he'd gotten the idea that it hadn't been an interruption but an end. Of course, for him, the scene had been interrupted, brutally interrupted, but the more time that went by, the more he was convinced that the encounter between himself and Vânia had had a beginning, a middle, and an end. It was a complete act. What he still couldn't understand was what that act meant. Or at least its full meaning. And something told him that this full meaning would arrive through Irene.

After describing his wanderings through Copacabana on the trail of Hugo Breno, Welber concluded by observing that the suspect didn't go out walking in order to do anything specific, but that he was walking just for the sake of walking. For him, walking wasn't a means, it was an end in itself. The strange detail was that Hugo Breno didn't walk just anywhere or in any specific way, but that he seemed to think it was essential to walk in the middle of the crowd. If there was anything he was looking for on his wanderings, it was the crowd. He'd seemed to Welber like an extremely solitary man. A hermit among the crowd, Espinosa commented at the end of the detective's story.

After hearing Welber out, Ramiro shared the conversation he'd had the same afternoon with Adélia Marques, a friend of Dona Laureta's, an eighty-two-year-old lady who lived in a hotel, thin, with elegant gestures, immaculately dressed and with her head square on her shoulders. She and Laureta had been friends for many years, when their husbands were still alive, and they'd stayed friends after their deaths. According to her, Laureta Sales Ribeiro was an intelligent and active woman. She didn't like television and she hated any activity designed for senior citizens. She had her own opinions about politics and economics and she never liked the government, whether it was on the right or the left.

"When I asked her if she'd ever heard Laureta mention a friend and neighbor whose son worked at the Caixa Econômica, she said that she knew who the friend was and that she'd even met her a few times. From Laureta, she learned that this friend had a very religious background, very morally strict, hardworking, and had been abandoned by her husband as soon as her son was born and had raised her son without any help from anyone. I asked her what she knew about the son. She said that she knew very little. The mother and son kept living in the same apartment until she died, about a year ago. The interesting fact is that Dona Laureta told her that the woman felt very guilty about her son. Dona Laureta didn't know why, she just knew that it was something that caused her enormous suffering. That was the mother of Hugo Breno, our suspect. The lady didn't remember anything else about his mother. As for Laureta herself, she told her friend she remembered lots of things, but that it would come back to her slowly; she couldn't remember everything at once."

"And the other friend?" Espinosa asked.

"According to Adélia Marques, she's senile, she hardly remembers anything, and she can't even form a complete sentence. The only one alive who's still in her right mind is her."

"Things are starting to make more sense," Espinosa said, "mainly because we're starting to see a connection between Dona Laureta and the suspect. A decisive contribution might come from the newspaper archives Detective Chaves is researching. Keep an eye on Hugo Breno when he's not at work. He has to meet someone. Nobody can be as solitary as he seems to be."

It was lunchtime and neither Vânia nor Irene had called. Espinosa was starting to think that Irene wouldn't find out about her friend's visit to his apartment. Or, if she had found out, she would have sent Vânia packing back to São Paulo, and was mulling over ways to punish Espinosa. The scene of Achilles dragging Hector's body through the dust and throwing it to the dogs to be devoured came to mind. He didn't like the image. But he also didn't think that Irene would try to pull an *Iliad* scene with him in the role of Hector. He went out to lunch.

That afternoon it was Ramiro's turn to follow Hugo Breno. At a quarter to five, he stood in a store on the other side of the street from the Caixa Econômica, waiting for Hugo Breno to come out. At five-ten, the bank employee emerged from the staff entrance and took a left down the sidewalk of Barata Ribeiro. Ramiro left the store and walked down the opposite sidewalk, parallel to him. He'd hardly walked a block when, in Cardeal Arcoverde Square, Hugo Breno went into the subway station. Caught by surprise on the other side of the street, facing heavy traffic, Ramiro had to wait to cross the street, giving Hugo Breno an advantage that could end his mission right then and there. When he finally managed to pass through the cars and enter the station, he saw Hugo Breno already on the other side of the entrance, and Ramiro didn't have a ticket. There was a small line in front of every ticket booth. If he waited his turn, he would risk missing the train Hugo got on, and Hugo had already disappeared deep into the station.

Ramiro ran up to the entrance, flashed his badge, saying it was an emergency, and jumped over. He ran down the first escalator, crossed the long hallway that led to the second escalator, ran down it, and did the same thing on the third escalator, until he reached the platform. The number of people waiting for the train indicated that Hugo was most likely still there. He looked to the right, where there was less room, and didn't see him. The left side was much longer and was full of people. He walked along the wall eyeing the people waiting on the edge of the platform. He wouldn't have a second chance. Either he would find Hugo Breno immediately or he would have to get into the last compartment and walk through the entire train, easy enough to do off-peak but unfeasible during rush hour.

He heard the noise of the train approaching, saw its headlights, and then spotted Hugo Breno in the middle of the small crowd that was pressing forward on the platform. He took up a position likely to be near the other door to the same car and waited for the train to stop and the doors to open. He pressed his way through and managed, after much pushing and shoving, to get into the car he wanted but, distracted by the struggle, he couldn't confirm that Hugo was in the same car or even if he'd stepped onto the train or still waited outside on the platform.

As soon as the doors closed and the train started moving, Ramiro kept his gaze trained out the window, in the anxious expectation of seeing Hugo Breno calmly walking down the platform. He didn't. Which meant Hugo was in the train. He scanned the faces in the car as the train headed toward Botafogo station. That was one of the longest distances between stations, which gave him time to locate the suspect. Moving slowly through the packed car, pretending to make his way toward the exit, he managed to spot Hugo in the middle of the car, standing in the thickest concentration of passengers. Ramiro stayed next to the door, in case he suddenly had to go out after him. But Hugo didn't get off at Botafogo. Instead, many more people boarded, making any movement inside the car impossible. The next five stations went by, but Hugo didn't move. When the train left Cinelândia station, Hugo started moving slowly toward the main door of the car. Ramiro was already next to the other door, tracking his every move. As soon as the train stopped at Carioca and the doors opened, both of them stepped onto the platform at the same time. Hugo moved toward the nearest escalator and went out onto the Avenida Rio Branco.

Not only was Carioca station one of the busiest points on the subway line, but the Avenida Rio Branco, in the late afternoon, hosts one of the most dense concentrations of people and vehicles in the entire city. Ramiro couldn't take his eyes off Hugo for a single second without risking losing him entirely. Further complicating his efforts, Hugo always seemed to choose to walk exactly where the most people were. He didn't try to move past or avoid people, instead maintaining the same pace for several blocks. When he got to the corner of the Rua Sete de Setembro, he turned left toward Uruguaiana. Once there, he turned right and walked one block down Uruguaiana, returning to Rio Branco via the Rua do Ouvidor. Halfway down Ouvidor, Ramiro lost sight of him. Hugo was a few steps ahead of him and then suddenly disappeared. He couldn't have turned around, since Ramiro would have seen him. . . . Maybe he'd picked up the pace and headed into some gallery, though that would be unlikely, given his actions up to that point.

Ramiro was walking in circles—not an easy maneuver—and looking in every direction when suddenly Hugo Breno walked right by him coming from behind, almost bumping into him, still heading toward Rio Branco. Ramiro followed more closely, taking the chance of being discovered. Which, judging from the circumstances, had already happened. Back on Rio Branco, Hugo walked one more block and turned left again onto the Rua do Rosário, and continued up to Uruguaiana, returning once again to Rio Branco. And that's what he did, followed by a despairing Ramiro, until he reached the corner of Rio Branco and Presidente Vargas: nine or ten blocks as the crow flies, or about fifteen blocks in Breno's zigzag pattern. All this during the busiest hour of the day in the middle of town, when people were getting off work. At no point did Hugo Breno stop to go into a store, look into a window, speak to anyone, or even appreciate that mass of moving humanity. What stunned Ramiro the most was that as soon as he got to the corner of Rio Branco and Presidente Vargas, Hugo turned around and redid the whole trip in reverse, taking the same side streets, all the way back to Carioca station, where they'd begun.

On the way, Ramiro lost sight of him a few times, until he'd suddenly appear out of nowhere, as if he'd been playing hide-and-seek with the inspector. At Carioca station, they went down the escalator and waited on the packed platform for the train to Copacabana.

The journey had begun in broad daylight and finished up at night. It was almost eight when Ramiro left Breno at his home, not having seen him speak to a soul during that whole time. The inspector was convinced that Hugo Breno wasn't interested in people or whatever was around him; he didn't look at anyone or pay attention to the traffic or to buildings while he was walking. He derived pleasure from being among the crowd, as Welber had observed the day before. He didn't bump into people, except accidentally. He liked being among them, without touching them. He wasn't a groper or a voyeur. People, individually, didn't interest him.

Espinosa's meeting with his team ended after seven that night. As soon as the group broke up, Welber and Chaves approached to tell him that Detective Chaves had finished his inspection of the newspaper archives.

"What did you find?" Espinosa asked the detective.

"Not much, boss. The tough part was the word 'murder.' I focused the search on news about murders and murdered children, but I didn't find anything connected to the Peixoto District or to Copacabana. I only got something by crossing the obituaries with the local news. I wrote up what I found."

Espinosa took the printed page with Chaves's summary: "In January 1975, an eleven-year-old girl was found dead next to the stairwell leading to the roof, inside the building she lived in, located in the Peixoto District, in Copacabana. The girl had a bruise at the base of her cranium, suggesting that she had fallen from high up in the stairwell and hit her head on the side of one of the stairs. The bruise, followed by an intercranial hemorrhage, was the cause of death. There were no markings on her legs or arms. The door leading onto the roof was closed with a padlock. It was not possible to discover if the girl was alone in the place or what she was doing on the stairwell that led up to the roof. There was no police description of the accident." Chaves waited for the boss to finish reading and added:

"I noted the address on this piece of paper. They didn't publish the name of the girl or of her parents."

"Thanks, Chaves. Good job."

The policemen at the station, familiar with the chief's laconic manner, knew that a phrase like that amounted to high praise, and the young detective went away grinning from ear to ear.

The address indicated that the girl had lived less than fifty meters away from Espinosa's own building. When he went home, Espinosa walked by the building, trying to uncover some hidden memory, but he decided not to visit until the next morning, in daylight. That night he wanted to catch up on some reading, including Montalbán's latest book. Except if Vânia called suggesting a striptease, he thought. But Vânia didn't call or turn up. There was no striptease. He read a few dozen pages.

He got up a bit later than usual the next morning to give the inhabitants of the neighboring building time to leave for work without having to bump into a policeman poking around the premises. He called the station, saying he'd be a bit late but that he expected to be in the office by around ten. On the short walk to the girl's building, he was greeted by two people. He was well known in the Peixoto District. Since he'd already located the building the day before, he didn't have to confer with any doormen. The only precaution he took was to check if the addresses had changed in the last three decades. They hadn't. And the building in question corresponded vaguely to the one suggested in his murky memory. It was a building only three stories high, without an elevator or a garage, just like his own and all the area's original buildings. There was no doorman. There was a guard who kept an eye on that building and two others. Espinosa was informed by a resident that the guard was named Onofre and that he was probably in the next building at the moment. The chief had to ring twice before a man appeared, not in the doorway but in a narrow lateral hallway that led to the back part of the building. He was short and strong, with a creased face, white, short-cropped hair, and an attentive gaze, between sixty and seventy years old.

"Good morning," Espinosa said. "Are you Mr. Onofre?"

"I am," he said in a deep, hoarse voice that still had a trace of a northeastern accent.

"I'm Chief Espinosa from the Twelfth Precinct."

"I know. I know you from here in the neighborhood."

"I need your help, Mr. Onofre."

"I'll do whatever I can, sir."

"How long have you worked here?"

"Ever since there was a bamboo grove in the square. More than forty years. I got here when I was twenty-three and I'm about to turn sixty-five."

"Always in this building?"

"This was the first one I took care of. Then I started working in the next one and then in that one over there, with the green fence."

"Do you remember an accident, a long time ago, more than thirty years back, with a little girl here in the next building? She died after having fallen down a staircase. She hit her head. . . . I don't know her name."

"I don't know either," the man said, "but I remember the accident. It was horrible—the parents couldn't stand to keep living here and moved a month later."

"Would you mind showing me where it happened?"

"Of course, Chief. Right away. I'll go get the keys from my room."

Onofre was wearing some pretty ragged jeans, sandals, and a checked shirt with the sleeves rolled up to his biceps. Despite his age, he didn't wear glasses. He came back with a key ring. They went around the low wall separating the two gardens, and he opened the front door of the next building—which was an exact twin of the one they had just seen. The buildings in the Peixoto District were all very similar, in Portuguese colonial style, all three stories high. The only thing that separated them were their details and their colors. As soon as they walked into the lobby, Onofre pointed up the marble staircase and said:

"That's not where she fell, it was all the way up . . . as if she was going to the roof."

The guard went up on ahead, noting any disorder. He closed the lid of a garbage bin, picked up a piece of paper, and put it in his pocket. But the building was clean, the walls were neatly painted, and the floor was well taken care of. When they got to the last floor, he pointed to the staircase that went a bit higher.

"This is the last floor, but the stairs go up to the rooftop."

There were two more L-shaped flights, with a landing between the first and second. He stopped, with Espinosa, on the landing.

"Here's where she fell. She must have fallen from up there and knocked her head on one of the stairs."

"Was she by herself when she fell?"

"Since nobody saw her fall, nobody could say."

Espinosa went up the last few stairs, which ended on a little landing a couple of feet square, bordered by a low wall, beside the door to the rooftop. The watchman went up and opened the padlock. The terrace ran along the back half of the building, where the water tank was; the front half was covered with ceramic tile. Espinosa wasn't interested in the terrace, since it had been closed when the accident occurred. They went back down the stairs, and the door to the roof was locked once more.

"What floor did the girl live on?"

"The top."

"Onofre, I'd like to stay up here by myself for a few minutes. When I'm done, we'll talk some more."

"Fine, Chief. When you're done, just knock on the front door."

Espinosa went back to the landing between the two flights of stairs and looked up. What he saw was the final flight ending in the little landing and the door. He counted ten stairs, including the upper landing. If the girl had fallen from the last step, the fracture at the base of her skull would have been the final blow after she'd fallen, stretched out on the landing where she was found. The question was: What was she doing on those stairs? She knew that there was nothing more up there except the rooftop terrace, and that it was sealed with a padlock. If she had gone up those stairs, it was because something had attracted her attention. What? What made her fall? What could she have seen that frightened her? Had she been frightened and then fallen or had she been pushed? Espinosa sat on the floor and looked up. He thought: The girl goes out of her apartment and closes the door without making any noise. Just out of habit, since her mother's told her so many times not to slam the door. As she moves toward the stairs, she hears something in the area that leads to the roof. . . . She stops, quiet, attentive. After a few seconds, she hears something else, perhaps a whisper. She stays where she is, silent, and even more alert. . . . After a few more seconds, she hears a noise and what appears to be a soft voice. . . . It could be a child's voice, or a woman's. . . . She tiptoes over to take a look at the first flight of stairs. Empty . . . and dark . . . another whisper. She goes up the first flight, sticks her neck around to see the rest. . . . The noise continues. She goes up the last flight and sees . . . what?

8

For the rest of the morning, Espinosa tried to construct a profile of Hugo Breno. Though they were all referring to him as a suspect, they really didn't have enough clues to justify that label. Espinosa had coined a term, contradictory in its redundancy, for situations like that: Hugo Breno was "suspected of being a suspect." A borderline state of suspicion. The only thing Espinosa and his assistants had on Hugo up to that point was that he had talked to the victim a few times, which was itself very natural, since he was a teller responsible for dealing with pension recipients and Dona Laureta was one of the pensioners who got her payment at the branch where he worked. Besides that, he could, at most, be considered a weird guy. But Espinosa himself was considered a weird guy by many of his colleagues. A few thought the more adequate term was "eccentric."

"But, Chief, he is really strange," Ramiro was saying. "I followed him for almost three hours through the streets of downtown without seeing him pause for a second to rest, to go into a store, or speak to a soul, or even to stand there and watch the world go by. Nothing, Chief. And there's more. Sometimes he would disappear. Just vanish. All of a sudden, he'd be right next to me, almost taunting me, as if to say, 'Here I am.' How did he do that? There's no doubt he's weird. He's like a robot, an automaton, loose in the streets of Rio de Janeiro. What Welber saw the day before yesterday, I saw yesterday. He's not normal."

"I know. But you also found out that he's an exemplary employee, efficient, that he doesn't cause problems. . . . So what's the conclusion? Is he normal or not?"

"A person can be normal at work and abnormal when dealing with other people outside of work."

"And how does he act outside of work? Does he bother anyone on the street? Does he get upset? Did he use violence at any point? Did he suddenly start to scream? Did he get lost in the middle of the street and not know what to do? Not know how to get home?"

"Chief, none of that had to happen for him not to be considered normal."

"We're not psychiatrists, we're cops. Those things might be similar, but they're not identical. We don't have to find out about his mental health, we have to find out whether he did or didn't commit the murder. Of course we're all guilty of murder, but here we're only talking about a real murder."

Welber and Ramiro sat staring at Espinosa, thinking he was as weird as Hugo Breno. And he noticed.

"Fine," he said. "Let's admit that Hugo Breno is a weird guy, and I agree that the way he walks through crowds is odd, but let's not get obsessed by that. We don't have any proof, any clue, no matter how weak, that he pushed the old lady under the bus. But we have a series of small hints connecting the two. Or, based on what Ramiro discovered in Dona Laureta's address book, connecting the three: Laureta, Hugo Breno, and his mother, the mother being the common element. Instead of a love triangle, it's a murder triangle. What's missing, though, is an explanation for what that link means. Maybe that's what Dona Laureta wanted to tell us when she came to the station."

Espinosa didn't think it was the right time to add another angle, the death of the little girl, to the already fragile evidence they'd gathered. The accident had occurred over thirty years earlier and its connection with current events was suggested only by Espinosa's memory, which was even more obscure than the events themselves. Of course, that didn't keep him from exploring his childhood memories, it just meant that for now he preferred to keep to himself the little bits and pieces he was trying to sew together. Especially because he knew that memory helps us forget as much as it helps us remember.

His cell phone showed that Irene had called, probably during his conversation with Welber and Ramiro about the case of the pensioner (which, he thought, was turning into the case of the man among the crowd). He called Irene. Her phone was off. It was Friday, the night they usually spent together. But he wouldn't have been surprised if she had gone back to São Paulo with Vânia.

Or even if she'd gone to São Paulo and left Vânia in Rio. Or if the two of them had stayed in Rio. But the best thing of all would be if Irene was alone in Rio.

He didn't have lunch. At least, not a normal meal. He ate a sandwich with an orange juice in a coffee shop in front of the station. But instead of going back to work, he headed toward the Peixoto District, more specifically to a little room at the back of the building next door to the girl's. Onofre had just awakened from a nap.

"Just a few minutes," the guard said, "fifteen minutes a day after lunch. But how can I help you, sir?"

"You may be able to help jog my memory. I was a boy, only twelve, about the same age as the dead girl, and I've already forgotten almost everything."

"If I may ask, Chief, why do you want to remember something that awful from so many years ago?"

"Because I think it may be connected to something else awful that happened last week."

"I have a good memory. The main thing I do when I work is remember. What do you want to know, sir?"

"If there were any comments about the girl's death . . ."

"My memory is better for things I saw than things people said. I remember perfectly the girl fallen in the stairwell and her mother shouting. I remember that people were scared. But what they said . . . it's been a long time."

"Of course you can't remember what they said, but can you remember if there were any comments, rumors?"

"The people who lived in these buildings all knew the kids who played in the square. They all knew the girl. They were really sorry about her death and felt sorry for the parents, who moved right after the incident."

"Was there any commentary about whether it really was an accident?"

"I think there was a rumor that the girl hadn't been alone. But nobody saw anything. Her mother found the body. I got there as soon as she started shouting. There wasn't anyone else in the stairwell or in the lobby."

"Why didn't they call the police?"

"I think because the girl fell, because it looked like an accident. So they called the doctor. . . . But that's what I think now; I don't remember what I thought back then."

"Do you remember if back then you thought it was an accident?"

"It's hard to say. It's more than thirty years ago. Time mixes up your ideas."

"Do you remember having heard anything about the kids who played out in the square, any friends of hers?"

"I don't remember, Chief. They were kids."

Espinosa took leave of the watchman and crossed the square on his way back to the station, a bit uncomfortable about having given Onofre the impression that he was looking for someone responsible for the girl's death among the children. Though he was.

At the station, he called Irene back. A recording asked him to leave a message. He didn't. He went back to the monotonous job of dealing with paperwork and the most serious cases sent up from the reception area. It was past four in the afternoon. Welber was getting ready to follow Hugo Breno; Ramiro had finished checking out Dona Laureta's phone book. The next morning, it would be Ramiro's turn to get a bicycle and follow Hugo Breno's marathon down Copacabana Beach. Espinosa was still dealing with his paperwork when Irene called.

"Hey, babe. Been missing you."

"Me too. Are you in Rio?"

"I am. Vânia left. She went back to São Paulo this morning. She sends her regards and says she hopes you'll forgive her for everything. She didn't specify what 'everything' meant. Why don't we have dinner somewhere nice?"

"Good idea. Should I come get you at nine?"

"Great. Kisses."

Human beings must be badly programmed, Espinosa thought, remembering the latest events involving

Vânia, Irene, and himself. Unless Irene didn't know about anything. At five, he went to the conference room, where all the policemen from the precinct were waiting for him.

"Good afternoon. Let's start off with the day's news . . ."

At nine, Espinosa got out of the taxi in front of Irene's building. The temperature was pleasant and the weather stable. They decided to walk to the restaurant, only three blocks away.

"What do you think Vânia meant by 'forgive her for everything'?" Irene asked as they were walking.

"I don't know, she's the one who said it. . . . Maybe for disappearing last weekend . . . for scaring us like that. . . . She must have talked to you about that."

"She did. And she really did feel guilty about it."

"Then that's what it was."

"Exactly. And not *for everything*."

"I think she meant for everything she did that weekend."

"Right. Maybe."

"Unless she was referring to the night she came to my apartment."

Irene started. She looked at Espinosa with an ambiguous expression, part fright and indignation.

"Come on, Irene. I wondered what you two were

planning with that: testing me or testing Vânia. I think the first idea would be pretty naïve and old-fashioned. The second made more sense."

"Seems like you thought everything was quite natural."

"Not everything. Maybe it was exactly that *everything* that she was apologizing for. Of all the activities that can be interrupted, I think of coitus interruptus as one of the most unpleasant. Or was that also what you'd agreed to?"

"Espinosa, you can't be that cynical."

"Not cynical. Skeptical."

"Don't mince words, Espinosa."

"I'm not. The skeptic is fundamentally a critic."

"And . . . ?"

"I didn't go after Vânia. I didn't call her. I didn't act in any way that might have suggested that she could call me up at night and then ring my doorbell in the middle of the evening asking where the bed was. Vânia's a gorgeous woman. I'm saying that to emphasize that it wasn't just any woman who rang my doorbell. She knows perfectly well that she's irresistible. What did you two expect? That I'd sit there telling her police adventure stories and then return her to you untouched at the end of the night?"

"You think we planned this?"

"Not all of it. That's why she's apologizing. She might have really been sincere when she ran out of my bed. That might have been the test."

"What test?"

"To see if she could manage to sleep with a man. Maybe her first attempts were violent and traumatic, and that led to the idea of testing out a man she already knew who'd already been tested by you."

"Are you insane?"

"Almost. But I managed to get a grip. Anyway, tell her I accept the apology."

They got to the restaurant. They stood outside for a while, looking at each other, not wondering about the restaurant but about whether they should still have dinner together.

"Let's not ruin our dinner," Espinosa said. "We can keep talking while we eat. Today all I had was a sandwich. I'd hate to have to go back home alone without having eaten."

She didn't object. Even if only because her expressions of surprise and near indignation didn't seem real. Espinosa thought that Irene was more curious, to see where the conversation would lead, than actually upset. They went in. The restaurant looked comfortable, and people said the food was good. Even though it was nine-thirty on Friday night, there were still tables.

As soon as they chose their drinks, they resumed the conversation—on his initiative.

"I'm going to tell you what I think happened. You were always the one who emphasized that we were lovers, and not boyfriend and girlfriend or husband and wife. We like to be together. So that never excluded other encounters. I never asked you who you were going out with when you traveled, and you never asked me either. We didn't promise fidelity, except to our own feelings for each other. So the possibility of our being interested in someone else sexually was part of our relationship. When Vânia propositioned me and I accepted, I didn't feel that I was betraying you. I didn't think I was putting our relationship at risk. Vânia is an extremely pretty and attractive woman, like you; the difference is that you and I go back almost a decade. So Vânia doesn't represent a real threat to our relationship. I don't know anything about her sex life, but I imagine that her experiences with men have been traumatic. I also imagine that for that reason she's experimented sexually with women. I don't think that's a definitive choice, I think she's trying to remake the idea she has of men after that supposed negative experience. I think I was part of that attempt to reconstruct herself, just like I think that the effort was planned by the two of you. And please don't look so stunned, as if what I'm saying is coming straight out of the blue."

"I'm not stunned by what you just said, I'm stunned by the coldness with which you said it."

"What did you expect? For me to be happy about being a guinea pig in a therapeutic experiment planned by my lover and her friend? I might have felt honored, but that's not what happened."

"There was no plan. There was no premeditation.

There was a conversation . . . a hard one . . . in which she said that she didn't think she'd ever have the luck to meet a man like you. And I answered that it wasn't a question of luck but of decision. I think she understood that as a suggestion for what she did. I'm sorry."

Though the dinner passed without conflict, when they left the restaurant Irene asked Espinosa to walk her back to her place.

9

It was rare for Espinosa to wake up on a Saturday morning alone when Irene was in Rio. But it happened that morning. A legacy of the fire Vânia had set.

At breakfast, the cries of the boys playing soccer in the square diverted his attention. He set aside the newspaper and pushed his rocking chair up to the French window. The game was taking place on a little paved fenced-off area. There were two teams of five players each, all teenagers, all playing with an intensity worthy of a World Cup final. Except for the pavement, the game was exactly like the ones he'd played decades before, with the same dedication and the same shouting; all that had changed was that today there was no dust being stirred up from the gravel. As if he were looking into a file, Espinosa superimposed upon that scene other equally important memories of his life in the neighborhood. That was when he had the idea to take out the photo albums from his childhood, started by his parents and continued by his grandmother. There were two of them: one of them with pictures from his first year of life and another covering the subsequent years, until his fifteenth birthday, when the register was interrupted. There were pictures of birthday parties and of Christmas dinners and from trips and outings. Espinosa was interested in pictures from two birthdays: his eleventh and twelfth, which were the two years that followed his parents' deaths. The albums weren't kept on the bookshelves, but in the room that had been his grandmother's for nine years, and which, ever since she'd returned to her own apartment, had been used for storage. During the years they lived together, his grandmother celebrated his birthdays by having his neighborhood friends over for sandwiches, sodas, ice cream, and cake, and she recorded the events with the same camera that had belonged to her son. Despite the happiness with which she did so, she was not exactly a talented photographer (the possible reason for the interruption of the photographic records). The pictures Espinosa was looking for were in the album, but they were out of focus and blurry, and some had come loose. The group united around the table as the birthday boy blew out the candles on the cake was a smudgy shadow against the afternoon light. It was impossible even to recognize Espinosa himself, much less the others. But though the pictures didn't preserve the images of Espinosa's childhood friends, the albums clearly delin-eated two periods in his life: the pictures in which his parents were present and those in which they were absent.

From the death of his parents, Espinosa's thoughts turned to the death of the girl in the neighboring building. Two sad moments, the one closely following the other. The first was definitely indelible. The second, half-forgotten, returned now, forcing its way through his memory. He started to remember the girl's face, ever so vaguely. He remembered her build more than anything: she was a little pudgy and had pigtails. Maybe a frightened look. He couldn't be sure. Maybe the frightened look was his. He remembered his closer friends better. Slowly, the image of the boy that Hugo Breno had been was becoming clearer, or enriched with a detail here and there, but his inner life, what he was thinking, what he liked, remained a mystery to Espinosa. The boy also seemed to look scared. Espinosa thought that the fearful attributes he was assigning to the boy and the girl were a kind of shadow in his memory that loomed over them. There were happy moments playing soccer or riding their bikes; other moments were marked by sadness and fear.

Why fear? What were they afraid of? Or maybe the right question would ask what Espinosa was scared of just then. It wasn't exactly fear, he thought; it was the feeling of apprehension that precedes the discovery of something very intense. In the silence that comes before the scream, it's not the cry that frightens us, it's the silence.

The soccer match was over. The players left the field to the younger boys and gathered around one of the park benches, discussing the game in shouts—much different from the whispered conversations in little groups decades before at that same place, about the death of the girl, as if they were revealing a secret.

He returned to his newspaper, interrupted by the shouts of the boys. He read two or three pages without registering what he was reading. He got up and went back to the window to look out at the square, as if something had fallen onto the earth.

It was midmorning. He put on some old pants, tennis shoes, and a T-shirt and went down to the street. He walked slowly around the square, distracted. Almost arriving back at the point of departure, he crossed the street and entered the side door of the building that gave onto Onofre's room. Maybe he had Saturday off or maybe Onofre didn't have anywhere to go on his free days. He found the watchman sharpening his plant shears.

"Good morning, Mr. Onofre."

"Good morning, Chief."

"I don't want to interrupt your work."

"It's nothing, I'm just sharpening the shears—they're the most important tool I have for taking care of the gardens. Are you off today too, sir?"

"I am. But like you, I'm sharpening my tools."

The watchman looked at the policeman.

"And once more, I need your help," Espinosa continued.

"Whatever I can do to help, sir."

"I need some information about the girl's building."

"Yes, sir."

"Why is the door to the roof locked? Was it always like that?"

"It was already locked before the accident. We found out that the kids were going up there to play. It's dangerous. The edge is very low. Besides, there's the water tank. Some kid could have come up with the idea of looking through the trap door and fallen in. We thought it was better to lock the door."

"What did the kids do up there?"

"I don't know, sir. There's not much room. The front half is covered, and the back is almost totally taken up by the water tank. There's not much room left over."

"Had someone already surprised the kids up there?"

"Not that I remember."

"So how did anyone know they were playing up there?"

"I don't know, sir. Maybe someone in the building saw them go up there."

"The girl who died lived on the top floor. So it was easy for her to leave the apartment and go up there."

"That's true, and she could only have been seen by someone who lived on the same floor. There's only two apartments per floor."

"Are you sure that the door was locked before the accident?"

"Absolutely. I put the padlock on there myself. The same one that's there to this day."

"I'd like to go up there one more time. I'd also like to take the key to the roof."

"Of course, Chief." The guard took two keys from his key ring. "Here you go. This is the key to the lobby and this is the one to the roof. When you're done, just give me a shout."

Espinosa went out through the building's front entrance and entered the next building. After going up the three stories, he went to the last flight of stairs, where the door led to the roof. He unlocked the padlock. It was a Yale, old and very tough. The door opened with a groan. Once he passed the landing, there were two steps down to the rooftop. It really was a small area, like a hallway surrounding the water tank on three sides. At most, on a hot night, a couple could go spend a few hours up there, if one of them had the key to the lock. He went out and locked the door. The only light came from a little window above the middle landing.

Espinosa went down to it and sat on the floor, as he'd done the day before. And, sitting there, he looked at the last flight of stairs and asked the same question: What had the girl seen when she was going up that last flight? Something must have made her fall onto her back. A runaway dog? A cat? A big moth that flew out at her? It was possible, though unlikely in a building whose lobby door was always closed. The image of a large moth suddenly flying toward the daylight coming through the window could frighten children and adults, no matter how harmless the insect. And there were a lot of moths around here, because of the abundant vegetation on the surrounding hills. But the theory wasn't very convincing. There wasn't enough room for a moth to get in, just as there was no interior light, especially on the staircase, that would attract it. Another idea: people. The girl leaves the apartment, hears human noises, goes up without making a sound, and surprises and is surprised by someone. What would a person, adult or child, be doing hidden on that landing whose door was locked? Sex was the most likely answer. Adults wouldn't have any reason to be having sex in such a limited space, accessible to passersby. And if adults were caught in the act, they'd try to hide or disguise what they were doing. More likely, it was kids, less careful and less experienced, as well as more likely to get scared.

Once Espinosa accepted this hypothesis, another thought followed: for that fact to become a threat that would make the girl try to flee or get pushed, it would have to be threatening to the people involved, children like her who, surprised and recognized, would have gotten scared and pushed her, only to flee afterward. It was terrible, but possible, Espinosa thought bitterly. He sat awhile longer on the stairs, trying to exorcise his inner demons. It was an aberration to try to impute to an eleven- or twelve-year-old child another child's death. But that was what he was doing. And that horrified him. He couldn't imagine the girl rolling down the stairs accidentally. In that case, she would have had scratches, purple marks on her limbs, and the newspaper had specifically mentioned the absence of wounds. The image he'd constructed of the scene had the girl being pushed and hitting her head directly on the edge of a stair. A strong, angry push, which could have been given by another child of the same age. And that was what was so horrifying. Not just the possibility of that having happened, but the fact that he, Espinosa, was thinking about that. He was pushing the girl. He got up and went to give the keys back to the watchman.

Back in his apartment, Espinosa made another cup of coffee, put two pieces of bread in the toaster, and decided to restart his day. No more noise came from children playing and the newspaper was already half-way read, but even so he tried to act as if his day was just beginning. As he was doing so, an idea came to mind that he had to think about. Every time he remembered the child Hugo Breno trying to be friends with him in the Peixoto District, he felt a sense of strangeness and threat. And now he realized that it wasn't the memory of only that boy that was connected with that negative feeling but all of the kids he knew around the time of the girl's death. And that included himself. He felt something strange and threatening whenever he thought of the period marked by the girl's death. And now, more clearly than before, he himself was present in the scene, seeing the girl being pushed from the top of the stairs.

How had he managed to come up with such a clear picture? Was it the fruit of his imagination or a real memory? Whoever had pushed her, even without mean-ing to kill her, had killed her. And that threat hovered over all of them, no matter how much their memories had worked to distort the original event.

10

Why couldn't it have been a moth? The question nagged Espinosa for the rest of his Saturday, like a dog trailing after its owner. The difference was that just then the owner was afraid of the dog. What really made him uncomfortable wasn't the doubt the question implied. He didn't have any doubts about whether the girl had been scared by something sexual or by a moth. Despite the form, the question wasn't a question; there was no doubt, just the certainty: it wasn't a moth.

At the end of the afternoon, Irene called to suggest that they spend the night together, an idea he immediately embraced. Espinosa took up reading about Montalbán's latest travels, in an attempt to frighten off the ghosts that surrounded his rocking chair, so that he would greet Irene in a lighter mood. Despite his precautions, when he opened the door to her two hours later, Irene's question was right on the mark.

"What happened?"

"Why?"

"Because something obviously happened . . . something serious."

"Nothing happened. I mean, nothing today."

"And yesterday?"

"No. Nothing. Everything's fine."

"Baby, when we feel the need to say that everything's fine, that means everything's not fine. Why don't you tell me what's on your mind—because something's obviously bothering you—so that we can finally have a pleasant night together?"

"It's not easy. . . . Even though it happened over thirty-five years ago."

"Thirty-five years ago?!"

"Almost."

"To you?"

"I still don't know to what extent."

"Of course you don't, you were a child."

"Twelve."

"You're tormented by something that happened when you were twelve?"

"Those are the things that really torment us. Other things are just problems."

"And can you tell me about that thing?"

"That's the problem: the clarity I used to have for recalling things that happened so long ago."

Espinosa told her the story of the dead girl as best he could.

"And why are you worried about this after almost thirty-five years?"

He briefly told her about Hugo Breno, without mentioning the death of the pensioner.

"The first story is really sad; the second one is really interesting. But the first one is the one that bothers you."

"Both of them bother me. I was there for both stories. Which, for me, aren't two separate stories; they're
just episodes in my own story."

"You're haunted by the ghost of your childhood, but
you're also feeling stalked by a ghost today. Which is
interesting."

"What's interesting?"

"That man . . . Hugo. . . . He gets off on losing himself in the crowd . . . for no reason . . . for the pleasure
of the crowds. He's not a thief. He's not a murderer . . ."

"There's some doubt about that."

"How do you mean?"

"He's suspected of having pushed an old lady under
a bus."

"And why would he do that? To rob her?"

"No. That's the other problem. We couldn't discover
any motive for the crime."

"And did they see him push her?"

"No. Nobody saw anything."

"Espinosa, you've told me two ghost stories. In neither of them can you assure me that a murder took
place, and in neither of them do you have a murderer.
Two people definitely died. But how do you know they
were murdered? What's haunting you about these stories?"

"The fact that I can't distinguish between my real
memories and the memories that are superimposed on
the real memories and hiding them. I'm afraid I might
be using the image of the boy that Hugo Breno was to

hide another image, which would be the one of the true cause of the girl's death."

"And what real image might that be?"

"That's just it. It could be any of them. Including my own."

"Are you trying to tell me, Espinosa, that when you were twelve you could have caused the death of the girl?"

"It's a possibility."

"Espinosa, hon, why don't we do something concrete that feels good that also involves fantasy?"

The next morning, while they were having their coffee, Irene took up the conversation from the night before.

"Before I fell asleep, I was thinking about the man in the crowd. He's very interesting. You said that he lives alone, has no friends, no wife, doesn't talk to anyone, and that he gets his thrills by mingling in the crowd."

"Right. But be careful not to romanticize him. We call him the 'man of the crowd' because of the Poe story, but he's nothing more than an employee of the Caixa Econômica who has some odd tics."

"Some odd tics? Babe, you have some odd tics. This guy is flat-out weird. But that doesn't mean he's not interesting. He's completely solitary, but his greatest pleasure is to spend hours in the middle of the densest crowds, and during all that time he doesn't speak to anyone, he doesn't touch anyone. And you think he tossed the old lady under the bus? And you think that when he was eleven he threw that girl down the stairs? Is it because of the modus operandi that you're connecting the two?"

"In . . ."

"Sorry, honey, that was in bad taste. Let's not talk about the man anymore."

They didn't speak of Hugo Breno, just as they didn't speak of the girl, but that didn't mean they weren't thinking about them, feeling that the strange story of the two characters was present as a subtext in everything they were saying. Sunday ended without invoking noteworthy emotion, bathed in the soft autumn light that was coming through the French windows.

Monday morning. Overcast, temperature dropping, rain predicted for the afternoon. It wouldn't be as hot, and that was fine with Espinosa. He put his newspaper aside and went to get dressed. It was eight-ten in the morning and he wanted to be at the station by eight-thirty.

Monday morning isn't just any morning; it's a kind of symptom of the weekend. Instead of arriving rested up and happy to get back to work, people got in late, as if Saturday and Sunday had unleashed a massive sociocultural hangover. Ramiro and Welber hadn't avoided the syndrome of the first day of the week.

"Morning, Chief, you called us?"

"That's right. Which of you is going to follow Hugo Breno this afternoon?"

"I am, boss," Welber said.

"Then, Ramiro, you're going to go speak with Dona Adélia, Dona Laureta's friend. She said that she couldn't remember everything all at once. You were with her last Wednesday. It's time for her to try to remember something else. See what you can find out about Hugo Breno's mother."

Ramiro's best weapon in interviews was managing to get close to the person he was interviewing, like a cousin who had been missing for years, or an old neighbor. People who resisted talking to the police, after half an hour talking to him, would start confiding in him as if he were a childhood friend. And since that favorable climate had already been established on a previous visit, the eighty-two-year-old lady, who had dressed up to receive the visitor, came down to talk to Ramiro in the lobby of the hotel where she lived. The hotel was only a block away from Catete Palace. It wasn't a big hotel: not five stars or even four; some guidebook might have awarded it three at the most. But it still retained a few traces from the old days, when it had been a sought-after location for politicians from other states in town for meetings in the palace, back when Rio de Janeiro was still the seat of the federal government.

"Good afternoon, Inspector, how nice of you to come back."

"It's my pleasure, Dona Adélia. The only reason I didn't come earlier was so as not to bore you with police business."

"But we've never talked about police business . . ."

The discreet elegance of the lady could also be felt in the way she spoke and listened, and even in her impenetrable solitude. She didn't complain about anyone, she didn't mourn the loss of anything, and she seemed to look for her pleasures in the slightest facts of everyday life. The conversation with Inspector Ramiro was certainly outside her everyday life.

"I feel like you are looking for something, sir, but I can't quite tell what it is."

"I myself don't know exactly what I'm looking for. I just know that it has to do with the strange death of Dona Laureta and with Dona Alzira, Hugo Breno's mother, the one who works at the bank. Do you know what she died of?"

"All I know is that it was sudden. As far as I can remember, she wasn't sick. You know that after a certain age the favorite subjects of conversation become illness and medicine."

"And Dona Laureta didn't have any serious illness?"

"No. Nothing serious, at least. She was a bit nervous, but that was all."

"How do you mean, nervous?"

"She was . . . it's hard to put my finger on it. . . . She was electric, agitated."

"And Dona Alzira?"

"I knew her less; she wasn't exactly my friend, she was a friend of my friend Laureta's, but we did see each other sometimes. Since the three of us lived nearby, we did sometimes run into each other at the grocery store or even at the market. She was a strange person."

"How do you mean?"

"A bit wary, not too friendly, but when she spoke she did sometimes reveal things about her private life. She didn't reveal anything as a complaint; it had something to do with her religion, something moral, as if she was permanently doing battle with something."

"Do you remember any of those revelations?"

"Not exactly about the revelations specifically, but about the theme, which was always about her son and her worries about him. Which frightened me, because her son was a strong, healthy, grown-up man, with a good job at the Caixa Econômica. . . . I didn't understand what she was so worried about."

"And she didn't say?"

"From what I could make out, it wasn't anything that affected her son directly, but it was something to do with her, though it also had to do with her son. It was a complicated situation. Her son, she said, didn't complain about anything; she was the one who complained, as if there was something wrong with the son that she felt but he didn't. It wasn't a sickness, it was some kind of guilt she had in relation to her son. Hard to understand."

"Did she die in an accident?"

"No. I think she died of something that came over her suddenly. It might have been her heart, though I can't remember her saying that she had anything wrong with her heart."

"And her son, did you ever meet him?"

"No. I saw him once or twice, but from a distance. We never spoke."

"You also said that none of the three of you had any serious illness, despite the minor complaints of old age. Was there any possibility that your friend Dona Laureta might have had a serious illness and not told you about it?"

"No. If she'd had something serious, I would have known. We were really close. . . . And we didn't have that many other people to talk to . . . except our doctors, of course."

"Do you think your friend could have killed herself?"

"No. Definitely not. When I said she was nervous, I didn't mean that there was anything wrong with her mentally. She was someone who was always busy doing things, she was jumpy, but not at all crazy. She'd never have committed suicide. You can be sure that she didn't throw herself in front of that bus."

The interview continued a little while longer, but Ramiro knew that the chances of obtaining any more useful information were small. He made a few more comments and then brought the conversation to a close. The old lady's confidential assurances that her friend would never have committed suicide seemed to have more to do with her than with her friend. Nobody could guarantee that another person would never commit suicide, especially when that person was eighty years old and had lost her husband and all her relatives. The two bits of information that might possibly be useful were reaffirmations of what she'd already said, both about Dona Alzira, the bank teller's mother.

Since the interview was shorter than he'd expected, Ramiro decided that before going back to the station he'd try something else in the building on Siqueira Campos where Hugo Breno lived. The Catete subway station was only one block from the hotel where he was, and the Siqueira Campos station was itself only a block from Hugo Breno's building. It couldn't have been more convenient.

The three-story building had been built on a lot that wasn't more than six meters wide and was limited at the back by the Rua Santa Margarida. In front, there was just a double door and a little hall that ended in a stairwell. There was no lobby, strictly speaking, just a doorbell outside. Ramiro rang a few times and waited for a long while. He was about to leave when he saw a man come out whose status was not immediately apparent. He wasn't wearing a uniform, but he didn't seem to be a resident either.

"Good morning, are you the doorman?"

"I can help you."

The building didn't have a doorman; instead, it had a kind of watchman who also cleaned and did some electrical work. He'd worked on the construction of the building when he was still very young, and had come back years later in search of a job. They didn't have anything regular to offer him, but they needed someone to do some cleaning and small odd jobs. He accepted and never left. He'd never had a clearly defined job. He wasn't the doorman, but he also wasn't the custodian. He said he was the watchman. He wasn't a regular employee of the building. He got a salary contributed to by the tenants and he lived in a room that had originally been a storage area. The provisional situation had now lasted twenty years. All this was told to Ramiro by the man who called himself the watchman, after Ramiro asked if he was the doorman.

Ramiro thanked him for the information and asked his name.

"People call me Pernambuco."

"I'm Inspector Ramiro, from the Twelfth Precinct. I need to talk to a lady who they said lives here. She's a widow with a son who works at the Caixa Econômica."

"That could be Dona Alzira from the first floor . . ."

"Does she have a son who works at the Caixa?"

"Yes, sir. . . . But the problem is that she died."

"She died? A long time ago?"

"No. Last year."

"Do you know what she died of? She was in such good health."

"She sure was. It was sudden. One day she was fine, the next day she was dead. Her son said it was her heart."

"And the son, does he still live here?"

"He does. The apartment's his."

"And what's he like?"

"Quiet. He hardly says a word. He must have been sad when his mother died. . . . That's what I think. . . . But he was always like that."

"Like what?"

"Quiet. He doesn't talk to people. He only says what he has to say, and nothing else."

"And did he get along well with his mother?"

"That I don't know, sir."

"Did you notice anything strange between them?"

"Between them, no. What I thought was strange was that one day after his mother died he spent the whole afternoon burning her things. He called me and told me to give her clothes to whoever I wanted. And I saw on the living-room floor a big pile of papers, notebooks, all with stuff written on them, which he was tearing up and putting into a big metal bucket. Later I saw him light it all on fire. I mean, I didn't see him do it, but since he lives on the first floor I can see his outside area. Smoke was coming out of there the whole afternoon. And I saw him throwing bits of paper into the bucket."

11

Welber got to his observation post half an hour before five and stood waiting for Hugo Breno to emerge for another one of his plunges into the crowd. Even though he was prepared for any adventure, Welber ardently desired for the man not to repeat his downtown tour, nor go out in search of new crowds; instead, he hoped he would remain in Copacabana, more accessible, without any extra complications with the subway. At five to five, Welber focused on the revolving door of the Caixa branch. Five o'clock. One minute past . . . two . . . three. . . . The detective checked his watch against the clock in the shop where he was: five past five. Something must be keeping Hugo Breno in the bank. Quarter past. Maybe he hadn't closed yet; maybe he was a few centavos off and he couldn't leave until they spotted the error. Five-thirty. No, it had nothing to do with the cash box; maybe he'd fallen ill. Six o'clock. All the lights went out and the door of the agency was locked. Hugo Breno hadn't come out for the simple reason that he wasn't inside.

Welber went straight to the building where he lived, on Siqueira Campos, and rang the bell. When the man who answered heard the question, he said:

"Your colleague was already here this afternoon asking about his mother."

"My colleague? Asking about his mother? She's dead."

"That's what I told him."

"Did my colleague give his name?"

"I think it was Ramires."

"Ramiro. Inspector Ramiro."

"That's it. If he's an inspector, he ought to know that the man's mother's dead."

"That's true, but I'm interested in him, not his mother."

"I haven't seen him. Not yesterday or today. I think I didn't see him the day before either."

"He took advantage of the weekend and disappeared."

"So to speak. Maybe he took a trip. I didn't see him with a suitcase. But I didn't see him without a suitcase either."

"If he shows up, no matter what time it is, call me. My name is Welber. This is my cell phone number. You can call collect."

Welber went back to the station. He was sure that he hadn't let the target escape. There was only one door to the Caixa. There was no back exit or internal access to the upper floors of the building. And Hugo hadn't gone out the front door. He'd return to the bank the next morning to see if Hugo Breno had left before four-thirty. Meanwhile, he'd have to tell Espinosa that the suspect had disappeared.

"Disappeared? What do you mean?"

"I don't know, boss. I got there at four-thirty. He always leaves right at five. I waited until they'd locked the doors and turned out the lights. He didn't show up."

"He might have taken advantage of several people leaving at once to go out with a group, and you might not have seen him."

"There's only a revolving door. Only one person comes out at a time. And I was watching everyone who came out."

"Could he have left disguised?" Ramiro asked.

"Only if he was a master of disguise. And even then, why would he hide, if he could just walk out? And it's not just that. His building's watchman says he hasn't seen him since Friday. He fled."

"Couldn't he be on vacation?" Espinosa asked.

"That would be a big coincidence, Chief. Tomorrow morning I'll go back to the bank and see if he missed work, took vacation, or was out sick."

Ramiro, in turn, shared what he'd learned that afternoon, from Dona Adélia, the dead pensioner's friend, and from Pernambuco, the watchman in Hugo Breno's building.

In the first interview, the most important information related to Hugo Breno's mother; the second, with the watchman, covered Hugo burning documents, letters, and notebooks right after his mother died.

"I think his mother left some written record of her son's story and of the event that was causing him to suffer," Ramiro said. "I just wonder: How far did Hugo go in burning the records?"

"Are you thinking he killed his mother?" Espinosa asked.

"It's more of a feeling than an idea."

"Let's see what Welber finds out at the Caixa tomorrow. Depending on that, we'll put more pressure on him."

The next morning, Welber confirmed what they already suspected. Hugo Breno hadn't fled, he'd only asked to take some of his vacation days starting on Monday, thereby extending the holiday to Saturday and Sunday as well. So he was already on his fourth day of vacation, which meant that at that point he could be anywhere in the world.

It was almost eleven in the morning when Espinosa called Ramiro and Welber and asked them to close the door to his office so that they wouldn't be disturbed.

"I think we already have enough material to take a deposition from Hugo Breno . . . as soon as he comes back from his vacation, of course. Nobody knows where he went. But I think he'll be back. We won't call it a deposition, we'll just call it a preliminary procedure, and tell him that we're trying to gather information. Which is true. Meanwhile, there are a few facts that shouldn't be brought into the investigation, but it's important for you to know about them. What I'm going to tell you happened when I was twelve years old and the man we're investigating, Hugo Breno, was eleven. These memories started coming back to me after I saw what Chaves found in some newspapers from the period and after a few chats I had with a man called Onofre, who was, and still is, the watchman at a building where an eleven-year-old girl died. She was a neighborhood girl who played with us."

Espinosa recounted the girl's death in as much detail as possible, including the comments people made at the time and adding what Onofre had said about it, followed by his own suspicions about the involvement of a neighbor boy in the accident.

"But listen," he continued. "At the time, there was nothing to incriminate any of the kids in the group. There was nothing—and this I just realized—to suggest sexual violence against her. Everything suggested that the girl's fall was an accident. There were only rumors, stories, comments suggesting that she hadn't been alone. Thirty-something years later, a lady confides to a friend that she's got a terrible guilt on her mind, that she's suffering horribly because of a crime her son committed. That lady is Hugo Breno's mother. We were a group of about ten kids, which included, depending on the game, a few girls. It's impossible to say exactly what they were all like after so much time, especially because I was involved myself. I'm not trying to incriminate an eleven-year-old boy today who might have been involved in the death of a girl the same age, a death considered accidental. I'm just trying to put myself in the place of that boy to try to understand facts related to him now.

"There is no evidence that Hugo Breno is responsible for any of the deaths we've referred to. So it's possible that the three of us have been taken over by our own fantasies and that Hugo Breno, instead of being guilty, is just the victim of sick minds. Ours. For myself, I hope that's the case. Yet as policemen, we have elements that might add up to something that's not just a flight of fancy but a real story that's developed over the course of almost thirty-five years, involving three deaths. Hugo Breno, when he was a child, could have somehow been involved in the death of a girl; years later, as an adult, he might have found out that his mother knew about it and that she'd told Dona Laureta; months later, Hugo Breno's mother dies in unknown circumstances; after another year he kills Dona Laureta, getting rid of the only witness to his childhood crime.

"I've got to tell you that the more I try to clear up this story, the more mysterious and unlikely it seems. Its starting point—Hugo Breno, when he was a kid, causing the girl's death—as well as its conclusion—Hugo Breno pushing Dona Laureta under a bus—seem unreal to me. The motive, first of all. Why and how would an eleven-year-old kid kill his friend? Of course she fell down the stairs and hit her head on a marble step. Terrible, but probably an accident. In that case, why would there be that guilt? Similarly, even if his mother had started feeling guilty about the supposed participation of her son in that accident, why would that boy, more than thirty years later, kill an old lady who was close enough to dying of natural causes because of the simple fact that she'd heard his mother tell that story? The most realistic and factual version of our case is still uncomfortably strange. I'm afraid that it's less of a case than a collective delusion."

The three of them were seated, mulling over their own ideas, unsure what to say or do.

"Let's go to lunch," Espinosa suggested.

The three of them went to lunch, but not together, as if they all needed to be alone to think about what had been said that morning. Welber went home for lunch, which he'd been doing ever since he'd moved to Copacabana, because that way Selma could supervise his diet. Ramiro preferred to save money and get a sandwich and a juice at the bar across the street. Espinosa went to the trattoria.

After lunch, he left the restaurant, on his way back to the station by a different, and definitely longer, route. First, because he needed to think, and he thought better walking than when he was sitting down with his head resting in his hands, and second, because he wanted to check out the area around Hugo Breno's building. It was still cloudy and the temperature was pleasant. Espinosa went down the Avenida Atlântica, walked four blocks, turned right onto Siqueira Campos, and went up to the subway station, on the corner of the Rua Tonelero, where Siqueira Campos split into two streets, at the beginning of the Ladeira dos Tabajaras. The block to the right, farther down Siqueira Campos, was where Hugo Breno's building was. It wasn't a very attractive area, near a shopping center that had seen better days, full of sleazy bars and auto-repair shops and close to the entrance to the Tabajaras slum. On the next corner, only a few blocks from Copacabana Beach, there was a small, friendly hotel for foreigners in search of cheap accommodations that also housed natives who wanted a room and a bed, as in an inn, only a few feet from the subway station. A good place for someone to hide out for a few days. He went around the block down the Rua Santa Margarida and stopped right where the watch-man had seen smoke coming out of the back of Hugo Breno's apartment, which made the man suppose that he was burning his mother's papers. The short street ended up at the Ladeira dos Tabajaras, near a taxi stand. Espinosa realized that some of the drivers at the stand had recognized him. He went down the street toward Siqueira Campos and returned to the station. Maybe Hugo Breno had burned his mother's papers not because they were compromising but because they were useless.

Welber and Ramiro thought about all the possibilities for locating Hugo Breno. They'd do that after talking to his colleagues at the Caixa and with his managers. None of his fellow bank employees knew anything beyond what neighborhood he lived in, much less where he spent his holidays. Once the two policemen had exhausted all the possible sources of information, they then started considering hypotheses. They stopped as soon as they realized that all hypotheses were possible, which meant that there was no hypothesis. Hugo Breno liked crowds, but he lived completely alone. He could be spending his holidays in São Paulo or in an isolated cabin in the mountains. There was nothing they could do but wait for him to come back to the Caixa Econômica.

The case of Hugo Breno was obviously not the only one being investigated by the Twelfth Precinct, nor was it the most important. So during the two weeks the suspect spent on holiday, work in the station went on as usual, until Sunday, the day before Hugo was supposed to be back at work, when Welber got a collect call. It was Pernambuco, telling him that Hugo Breno had returned on Saturday night. If he'd come home, that meant that he'd be back at work the next day. Welber called Espinosa and the boss agreed that if Hugo was back home without making a secret of it, that meant that he'd be at the bank on Monday morning. There was no reason to detain him for an interrogation on Sunday afternoon.

12

Monday morning dawned with a hot sun, mercury rising. From his window, Espinosa had a broad vision of the blue sky above São João Hill. He'd just had breakfast and was checking the weather page to confirm what he'd already seen for himself: good weather with slightly rising temperatures. Even though he'd been born in Rio, he didn't like the heat of the Rio summers. He thought that winter was the city's best season. Nice days with a temperature around eighty degrees.

When he got to the station, Welber and Ramiro were waiting for him. He told them how to approach Hugo Breno in the bank and about the measures they needed to take with his superiors to make sure he was let off for the rest of the morning. The main thing was not to frighten him. They didn't have anything on him, only hints, and they didn't want to lose what little they had.

It was ten-thirty when Welber and Ramiro returned to the station with Hugo Breno. Though he was waiting for Hugo, Espinosa felt surprised and touched by having in front of him the man he'd played with when they were kids in the Peixoto District. The discomfort they both felt was palpable immediately. Of course Hugo knew who he was, and of course he knew that Espinosa also knew who he was. What were they supposed to do? Greet each other like old friends? Walk down memory lane? Talk about how the neighborhood and the city had changed?

Espinosa got up, greeted Hugo, and invited him to take a seat, saying, "You're not being detained or forced to testify. I think that Inspector Ramiro and Detective Welber made clear that you're just being invited to clarify a few things in this preliminary phase of the investigation. In case you don't feel like doing so, you can get up and walk out of here at any time."

"I don't feel that way at all. I'm ready to help you."

Hugo Breno sat down in the chair nearest to Espinosa, while Ramiro and Welber sat farther off.

"Great. Nothing we say here is being recorded, and we won't take notes either," Espinosa said. "If that becomes necessary, we'll do so at another time. We're investigating the death of an eighty-year-old woman, a retiree who drew her pension at the same Caixa Econômica where you work. Her name is Laureta Sales Ribeiro. This woman was helped by you in the morning and died beneath the wheels of a bus the same afternoon, in circumstances that have not yet been totally clarified."

"And you think I can help clarify them?"

"Can you?"

"Chief Espinosa, the police are paid to solve crimes,

not bank clerks. I don't investigate crimes and I don't commit them, if that's what you're suggesting."

"I'm not suggesting that you committed any crime at all."

"Then why was I brought here by two police officers, who picked me up at my workplace?"

"Because there are signs that your relationship with Senhora Sales Ribeiro was something more than the monthly encounters at the bank window."

"Then those signs are wrong."

"And there are others that suggest a connection between the lady and your own mother."

"And what does that have to do with her death?"

"That's one of the things we'd like to know."

"Are you insinuating that the death of Dona Laureta has something to do with the fact that she was friends with my mother?"

"I just said that she and your mother were friends."

"Just like she might have been friends with any number of other ladies. What could that incredible fact prove?"

"Probably nothing except that they were sociable people. But I'm not thinking about those other ladies, I'm thinking about Dona Laureta's relationship with your mother . . . and the kinds of confessions they might have made to each other."

"Chief, my mother was a very religious and very fanciful person. What she might have told an eighty-year-old lady, more than a year ago, and in what way that lady might have taken it can't be considered a serious sign of anything whatsoever."

"And what do you think she might have confided to her?"

"Anything possible about human evil."

"And could that include possible evils committed by her own son?"

"My mother died a long time ago. Even if she had told Dona Laureta something about me, why the devil, after so much time, would I go push that lady underneath a bus?"

"Maybe because of the devil . . ."

"What?"

"That's what you said: why the devil . . ."

"Officer, you can't be serious."

"But I am. Of course I'm not thinking that Lucifer himself ordered you to provoke the accident that took the woman's life. But there are all kinds of devils. I mean, there are the devils in religious allegories and there are the devils we carry around inside us. I believe more in the powers of the latter than in the former. I don't know which one you were referring to."

"I can't believe this is a police interrogation."

"And in fact it's not. It's a conversation that's intended to clear up any ambiguities that we've found with respect to your relationship to Dona Laureta."

"What kind of ambiguities?"

"About the nature of that relationship and about any participation you may have had, voluntarily or not, in the accident that provoked her death."

"In other words, if it was my demons or someone else's that caused the accident."

"That's a delicate way of putting it. . . . That's what allegories are for."

"Chief Espinosa, I don't think there's any question at all. . . . At the most, a few confused guesses about a woman's death, in which you don't know how to place me and you don't know how to exclude me. Besides, you're the one using allegories, trying to fill in the lacunae with this talk of devils and demons. I don't think you have enough material to start a formal investigation. If we're talking here, it's not because of fond memories of our childhood nor because you have some accusation against me. If you did, this wouldn't be a conversation, it would be a police interrogation. So let me suggest this: in the name of our childhood friendship, let's cut this short and do the interview again another time . . . if possible, without witnesses. . . . Especially if the conversation touches on our childhoods."

"Do you think it ought to?"

"That's fine with me. Unless you're afraid of your demons." Hugo Breno got up. "Have a nice day, Chief Espinosa. Good-bye, Detectives." And he walked to the door.

Ramiro and Welber automatically got up to stop

him, but Espinosa made a slight gesture for them to let him leave, which Hugo Breno did unhurriedly and without the slightest sign of indignation. As soon as he left, Espinosa said:

"He'll be back. He himself is going to take the initiative to seek us out. He needs to talk. And everything suggests that he's more interested in talking about the past than about the present. He's the one who brought up our childhoods; we didn't mention it. And I'm sure that he won't just want to talk about his own childhood but about mine as well."

"We wondered if you had known him because he lived in the Peixoto District too."

"We used to play together when we were eleven and twelve years old."

"You didn't mention that."

"I didn't know—or, rather, I didn't know if it was true."

Ramiro and Welber scratched their heads and looked at the boss.

"Did you ask him where he spent his vacation?"

"In a small town in Minas . . . in a monastery . . . meditating."

"Either he's in the middle of the crowd or he's retreating in a monastery. That's the man for you."

"I thought it was artificial . . ." Welber said.

"What did you think was artificial?" Espinosa asked.

"That cocksure attitude. Showing no sign of being intimidated. After all, there were three cops in this room, but it was like Ramiro and I weren't even here. He was only interested in you. I think he was expecting this and had prepared for the meeting."

"He didn't seem the slightest bit concerned about the supposed murder of the old lady," Espinosa said. "But he seemed very interested in opening the door to mentioning his childhood, and in so doing to get me on his side, on the same team. We're not dealing with a run-of-the-mill bank clerk here. He might have strange habits, but he's intelligent and articulate. Let's wait for him to get in touch. I have a feeling it won't take more than three days. If he hasn't come to us by Wednesday, we'll check in on him again."

On Wednesday, as soon as he got to the station, Espinosa found a small envelope on his desk imprinted with the logo of the Caixa Econômica. *To: Chief Espinosa.* No return address. Inside, a handwritten note: "We can meet outside the station, in a neutral place, for an open conversation, with no time limit. If you agree, have this same envelope delivered to my counter at the Caixa with a date, time, and place." The note was not signed.

Ramiro and Welber didn't think the boss should accept a request to meet alone with a possible murderer in a neutral place—which meant a place out of their control—for an undefined amount of time. What did he mean by "with no time limit"? That the conversation could last the whole day and go deep into the night?

"Chief, this man is a nutcase. All you have to do is consider how he acts," said Welber. "He's like a wind-up doll . . . a robot."

"He didn't talk like a nutcase."

"He won't be able to stay coherent for more than fifteen minutes. That's why he left. He knew that he couldn't stand up to a confrontation," Ramiro insisted.

"What do you think could happen? He's going to kill me? If he wanted to do that, he would have done it a long time ago. He doesn't want me to kill him, he wants me to recognize him as an equal. And for that I have to be alive. Don't worry, there's no danger."

"Chief, he pushed that woman under the bus, believe me. And we don't know what else he might have gotten up to during all the time he was in voluntary seclusion. Or what he did to his mother."

"There's no witness to say that he was responsible for Dona Laureta's death, much less for his mother's. I want to hear what he has to say. One of you can make me a reservation for two people in a little hotel in the Peixoto District, halfway between his building and mine. It's a discreet, quiet place. Make a reservation for the day after tomorrow, Friday. I want a room facing the street. Have the two beds replaced with two comfortable chairs and a table. The reservation should be made in my name. The manager knows me. Afterward, I'll pay the bill myself, when I leave. Not with money from the station. It won't be official. I don't want you two in the next room or watching from the building across the street. If he realizes that he's being monitored, that's when he could turn violent. If people ask for me, say that I had to go to the hospital for the day for some tests. You don't know the name of the hospital."

On that same Wednesday afternoon, Welber went over to the little hotel in the Peixoto District to see if they had a room available for Friday. When the manager learned it would be used by Chief Espinosa, he guaranteed that a room with the specifications requested would be available at ten on Friday morning. The manager had known Espinosa long before he became the chief of the Twelfth Precinct, situated only a few blocks away from the small hotel.

Before returning to the station, Welber checked the access to the ground floor from the two upper floors, as well as if there was a door connecting the room they'd be in with the neighboring room. He also assessed whether there was any possibility of someone climbing the outer wall and reaching the room's small balcony. He checked out every corner of the building, which wasn't hard to do, given its size; and he talked with the employees in charge of cleaning, asking how many would be working on Friday and about how the staff went about their routines.

Welber still hadn't spoken to Ramiro about whether to obey Espinosa's order to stay away from the hotel. The idea was to work together on a watch, in order to keep the situation under control. The challenge would be to get Espinosa to agree with the measure.

On Wednesday night, the whole Twelfth Precinct team mobilized to break up a conflict between dealers fighting over the drug traffic in Chapéu Mangueira Hill, in what had previously been the peaceful neighborhood of Leme, at the outer edges of Copacabana. On Thursday, the policemen were all sleep-deprived, including Chief Espinosa, who planned to go to sleep early, preparatory to his encounter with his former childhood playmate. In a brief note, Hugo Breno had accepted the meeting at the hotel.

Before bed, Espinosa reviewed the case of Hugo Breno—a case with a history and a prehistory. Espinosa had started to think that the prehistory—the events in his and Hugo Breno's distant past—might be extremely relevant to the recent events involving the old woman's death.

Though tired from the sleepless night before, he didn't feel like going to bed. It was still early. If he fell asleep right away, he would wake up in the middle of the night, which would be much worse than waiting awhile longer and going to bed when he was really tired. He thought about calling Irene, but he decided not to; depending on how the conversation went, he could end up even more wound up and wide awake. He lifted the first book from the pile waiting on the table beside his rocking chair and opened to the page where he'd left off. He closed the book again, looked at the cover, the title, and the author's name. He returned to the story, but he didn't remember what he'd read in the earlier pages. Tired, he thought. Too tense from the night before. Too much work piled up during the day. Eventually he stopped thinking and nodded off. He got up and went to bed, trying not to think about anything else.

Espinosa awoke in fright, as if an alarm had gone off, summoning all the light sleepers, tired people, skeptics, and loners for one more day of work. It was Friday. He took an almost-cold shower, contrary to his usual habits, in an attempt to eliminate the remains of the day before. At eight, he was on his way to the station. There was nothing else left to do to get ready. There was really nothing to prepare anyway; he knew perfectly well that he faced an unpredictable situation, that the conversation could just as easily devolve into a resentful lament as it could turn into a debate that could digress in any direction. It would be up to Espinosa to direct or redirect the conversation.

As soon as he got to the Twelfth Precinct, he issued orders not to be interrupted, neither personally nor by telephone, and decided that Welber and Ramiro were not to go to the hotel nor to wait nearby to offer him protection. Hugo Breno was a proven loner, and he wasn't a member of a gang. Anything that he'd try to pull would involve him alone, without outside help. Espinosa was armed and ready to defend himself against any physical aggression (which he thought highly unlikely).

They'd agreed to meet at ten o'clock in the hotel lobby, and he wanted to arrive a half hour early, to make sure that everything was in place, according to the arrangements he'd asked Welber to pass on to the manager.

At nine-thirty on a sunless morning, Espinosa went up the Rua Décio Vilares, in the Peixoto District, toward a three-story colonial-style building, white with blue windows and a palm tree in the front, where he'd stayed a few times for domestic and professional reasons. He was greeted by the manager, who discreetly notified him that the other guest had not yet arrived and invited him to see if the room was set up as he'd requested. Espinosa asked if any guest had checked in the previous night or the night before that and if anyone had showed up wanting to see a room. Finally, he asked if room service was brought by male or female employees. Then he walked through the two side entrances and the service area.

At ten, Espinosa was in the lobby of the hotel. At ten, Hugo Breno arrived. He was wearing jeans, tennis shoes, and a checked shirt, not tucked into his pants. He had nothing in his hands. Espinosa went up to him and introduced him to the manager as a friend. The manager took out the key to the room.

"Are you going to need another key?"

The two of them looked at each other, Hugo Breno shrugged in a sign of indifference, and Espinosa answered:

"Thanks, one is enough." Then, turning to the recent arrival, he added: "Shall we go up?"

13

The two chairs were facing each other, near the window and the door that went out to the balcony. There was a small table in the middle, between them. Hugo Breno examined the bathroom and the inside of the wardrobe, and only then chose one of the chairs and sat down. Up to that point, Espinosa had been standing, waiting for his interlocutor.

"Thank you for agreeing to this conversation, which I consider private and off the record," Hugo began. "I know that it's not normal procedure and I suppose you've agreed because we've known each other since we were kids. And also because you have nothing against me, except a few fragile suspicions."

"Right on both counts," Espinosa answered.

"So why are you trying to surround me, to the point that I had to take my vacation early so that I could think about what was going on, without a policeman watching me and asking questions all over the place?"

"Because, even though our suspicions are fragile individually, they add up to a disturbing picture."

"Disturbing for whom?"

"For us, the police."

"Can you give me an example of one of those disturbing suspicions?"

"I can. The fact that you told my officers that your verbal contact with Dona Laureta consisted of nothing more than was required to pay out her pension. You even recounted the words you exchanged. But the security cameras showed a much more extensive and apparently harsh conversation between the two of you. There's also the fact that other similar conversations had occurred in the three previous months. Another factor that we can't dismiss is that on the same day that you spoke and she died, she went to my precinct to talk to the chief, whom she didn't know; she wanted to say something she thought was very important, so much so that she wouldn't speak to anyone less than the boss. Since I couldn't see her, she said she'd come back later. Finally, we have the fact that Dona Laureta, before she went back to the station, died while she was waiting to cross the street on a corner of the Rua Barata Ribeiro, which might be considered an accident if it weren't for several witnesses who said that the woman seemed to have been pushed into the middle of the street. I'll agree that none of this incriminates you directly, but I'm sure you can agree that those are disturbing facts."

"Chief Espinosa, are you thinking that if two people exchange a few absolutely necessary words when one of them is withdrawing money and one of them happens to die, then that means the other one had to have killed her? I'm a teller in a bank that pays out state pensions. People go to the same bank every month, and in general they go to the same window, to collect their pensions. That lady had been getting her pension for years at my window. I've never talked to her outside the Caixa. Why would I kill her? And why now, and not last month, or last year?"

"I don't know. If I did, you'd be under arrest."

"Nobody saw me push her into the street. Someone could have seen me on the sidewalk on Barata Ribeiro, near where she died. That's on the way to my house. I walk down that street every day."

"It's not true that you only knew her from the bank. She was friends with your mother and the two talked frequently, and, according to information we've received, they were confidantes."

"We've already talked about that. Dona Laureta was friends with my mother. Not with me. She talked to my mother, not to me. I repeat that I never once spoke with her outside the bank."

"And inside the bank?"

"My job is to help retirees and pensioners. There are thousands of them. Those people aren't my friends and they don't come to chat with me. If you think that old ladies and old men are sweet people, friendly, lovely, nice, you're mistaken. They are neurotic, annoying, irritating, whiny, and aggressive. They are the last people I would want to talk to."

"Yet from what we've seen on the tapes, you two had conversations that were much longer than what was necessary to pay out her pension."

"I never spoke to her more than what was absolutely necessary."

"So . . ."

"So, Chief Espinosa, the one who talked more than necessary was her."

"So besides going to the bank to pick up her pension, she also went to talk to you. And it wasn't friendly, pleasant conversation."

"I knew you weren't going to let me down, Officer. . . . Now you're on the right track."

"She wasn't a nice old lady, she was a big bad wolf."

"You got it. She had been blackmailing me for more than a year. It wasn't much, nothing that would end in murder. It was just a shitty little bit of blackmail, tiny, annoying, dirty, which she applied in homeopathic doses, every time she went there, and that got her a little raise in her pension. Obviously that money came from me and not from the government. And she knew that. She knew that I couldn't pay with money from the bank, because that would show up at the end of the day, at the end of my shift."

"And what gave her that power over you?"

"Her conversations with my mother."

"With your mother?"

"The two of them were exactly alike. Only the styles were different."

"You're saying that your mother was blackmailing you too?"

"As I said . . . only the styles were different. Can we get some coffee?"

The two of them had been seated in the same position

since the beginning of the conversation. When Hugo Breno got up and looked out the window toward the street, Espinosa went to the balcony to do the same and took advantage of the moment to scan the street in search of any sign of Ramiro and Welber. But there was nothing more than a few residents walking down the sidewalks and some parked cars, and neither of them were inside those.

After a few minutes, they heard a soft knock on the door. A girl brought in a tray with a coffeepot, cups, and cookies. While they were drinking their coffee, the conversation revolved around the changes in the neighborhood since the days when the two of them played soccer in the square. Espinosa got the impression that his former playmate was a good debater, but that he wasn't able to keep up a casual conversation. Everything indicated that his social life really was null. There was no question that this was a man without friends who felt good only among the crowd. There was no room for small talk. The coffee was good and both had another cup. Each of them had a cookie before moving ahead.

"So you were saying that your mother was also blackmailing you."

"Not in the sense of threatening me or taking money, but in the sense of guilt-tripping me and trying to pass on to me the guilt that she felt herself. In our conversation at the station, you mentioned demons. Well, my mother was demonic. She was even worse than Dona Laureta, because she always did it under the cover of religion and her faith in the Lord. She was a bad egg."

"She was your mother."

"She wasn't anyone's mother; all she knew how to do was be a daughter. And the only father she recognized was God the Father. I don't know how she managed to get pregnant."

"Aren't you being too hard on her?"

"You have no idea how much and for how long she tyrannized and threatened me. A daily tyranny that started when I was eleven and only ended when she died."

"What did she die of?"

"Heart problems, the doctor said. An organ she never had."

"Were you there?"

"Yes and no. She died in her sleep, in her room. I was sleeping in my room. Only when I got up did I notice that her door was still closed. She always got up very early."

"How did you know that she was asleep, if you were asleep too?"

"I don't know. I just guessed. But you don't have to wonder about that. If I had been awakened by some noise from her room and noticed that she was having a heart attack, I probably wouldn't have done anything."

Espinosa didn't notice any agitation in his manner. What Hugo Breno was saying wasn't accompanied by any emotion. There was no sadness or coldness. What he displayed was indifference. After so many years of brainwashing, what had remained of his relationship with his mother wasn't love or hate, or the inexpressiveness of self-control; it was pure indifference. The tone of his voice didn't change with the import of the words he was saying. The words had meaning, but no intensity.

"You know that failing to call for help can also be considered a crime."

"Of course I know that. It so happens that I was asleep, and I sleep deeply. Our street is noisy, and I've never gotten up in the middle of the night because of a car horn, a motorcycle, or a gunfight in the slums. Even if she'd called for help, with her door and mine closed, I wouldn't have heard anything."

"You said that her tyranny began when you were eleven. What happened when you were that age?"

Hugo Breno didn't speak for a few seconds, as if deciding whether to answer, shifting in his chair and taking another cookie. Espinosa knew he would respond. What he didn't know was whether his hesitation was real or just playacting, to make his answer more dramatic. He reinforced the question by saying:

"We agreed that this would be a private conversation. I'm not taking notes, and this is not being recorded."

"These aren't easy things to say. Some because of their content, probably, though now, after all these years, they've lost most of their emotional charge. But what makes it hard is that I can't guarantee the truth of what

I'm saying. Even the details might be wrong or not entirely true. It would be impossible to reconstruct exactly something that happened so long ago. I thought about it night after night. Having gone back over every detail so many times, I can't be certain if the version I remember today coincides with what really happened. The only thing I know for sure is that you were involved in the story as well. In a way, you were there too."

"Where?"

"In the square . . . inside the building . . . playing on the sidewalk . . . playing soccer. . . . Everywhere we used to play."

"And what happened?"

"You know what happened. You're only asking me so that afterward I can't say that you were the one who put the idea in my head."

"Even if that were my intention, it wouldn't change the question. After all, the one who brought up a tyranny from the age of eleven was you, not me."

"I was about to turn twelve. You were about to turn thirteen. That difference of a year meant a lot, mainly because you were much taller than I was, which made the age difference seem even greater. That's why I hung out with the younger kids. I really was younger. No matter what I did, we'd never be the same age, just like we'd never be the same height. But I wouldn't have minded being younger if you accepted me as a friend in spite of that. I didn't just want to play with you, I wanted to be your best friend. I dreamed about that.

You were my idol. I wanted to be just like you. I paid attention to how you walked, talked, dressed. I spent hours in front of the mirror trying to be more like you. Of course it didn't work. That idea made me grow apart from the other boys . . . or made them grow apart from me. You didn't blow me off, you just didn't pay any attention to me; you didn't even notice me. So I started isolating myself. And I started to see that I was going to lose you and all my other friends. I started to try to rejoin the group—and everything was going fine. That's when the girl died."

The silence that followed made the noise of a vacuum cleaner in a neighboring room, the voices of the staff in the hallway, the water in the shower of another room, the cars on the street sound all the louder. The world reemerged in the prolonged silence of Hugo Breno.

"What happened to the girl?" Espinosa asked.

"I don't know for sure. I just know that she startled us."

"Who, the girl?"

"Right."

"Startled you and who else?"

"I don't remember his name. It was one of your friends. He was somewhat friendly with me as well, but more with you. We'd agreed to go to the roof of the building where the girl lived. From there you could see the bedrooms of a few apartments. You could see people without their clothes on. I'd never seen that, but the boy said that from there he'd already seen a man and a woman naked. He said that he saw the two of them grabbing each other and that he could show me. So we went up to the roof, but when we got there the door was locked with a padlock, which only made me more curious. But without the key, there was no way to open the door. I was about to go back down when he took my arm and said that we hadn't been able to see, but that he could show me how they did it. I said I didn't want to. Seeing was one thing, doing was another. And I didn't want to do it. I thought it was wrong. I was scared by his suggestion, even though I didn't really understand what it was. But in a way he was my friend. He said everyone did that, that adults did . . . that it was cool. It didn't matter that the door was locked, we could do it right there at the end of the stairs.

"Of course I don't remember if that was exactly what he said. I had suggested going down, but I returned to the landing next to the door. I still thought he wanted to do something wrong, but at the same time I was tempted by the idea of doing something that adults did that was forbidden for children. That's when he told me that the older boys had already done it. I asked him which ones. He said all of them. I said what do you mean, all of them. And he repeated: All of them.

"With the door closed, there was hardly any light on that last flight of stairs. I was scared, but he promised me that nobody ever came up there, only the watchman, and he was working in the building next door. To calm me down and convince me, he said that he could first show me how it went and then I could do the same thing to him. All I had to do was pull down my shorts and lean over the little wall. I was nervous and scared, but at the same time I was excited by the idea. I was so focused on what he was saying that I didn't even realize that we were in a place where anyone in the building could show up. What I remember with extreme clarity is that when he was doing it to me, I looked toward the stairs and saw the girl, two steps below, looking at us in fright. I was terrified, pushed my friend away, and ran down the stairs. I don't know which one of us knocked her over. Maybe it was me. I was the first one to run past her. We ran down the three flights and only once we were on the ground floor did he tell me that the girl had fallen down the stairs. We left the building without anyone seeing us. We swore that we would never tell anyone what had happened. Each of us went back to our houses, and I was very frightened. The next day, I found out that the girl had died when she fell."

Hugo Breno paused for a moment and then went on, in the same indifferent tone.

"You might be wondering how I can still remember all of this, after so much time. But the impressive thing is not that I can still remember it but that I've never managed to forget it. My mother also found out about the death the next day. She asked if I knew her. She said that she'd heard that the girl wasn't alone. She asked if I knew who might have been with her. I didn't go back to the Peixoto District for a few days. I came straight back from school and stayed at home, or I went to play in the Rua Santa Margarida, behind my building, where my mother could see me from the service area of our apartment. After I hadn't gone to the Peixoto District for a week, where I used to go every day, she started to doubt whether it was only that I was afraid to go back because of what had happened to the girl.

"That's when the interrogations started. For days on end, relentless. The questions came with all kinds of religious threats. That I was going to feel the anger of God, that if I didn't expiate my sin I would go to hell. That it was no use lying because God could see and hear. . . . She used everything she'd heard at church. The only way to save myself, she said, was to confess the truth and get rid of my guilt. Out of exhaustion and fear, I ended up confessing that I might have knocked the girl over accidentally. From that point on, she started telling me that I was the murderer of an inno-cent little girl, and that both me and her, my mother, would have to expiate our guilt in front of God. I don't have to say that I was doubly terrified. I thought that any minute now the cops could come knocking on my door, that my mother would turn me in, and that I would be arrested; and if that wasn't enough, I felt per-manently stalked by the punitive gaze of the Lord. I was only eleven. I didn't have a father. I didn't have any relatives I could go to. And I was afraid of priests, pas-tors, bishops—all kinds of clergy. As time went on, she started using emotional blackmail, intending to control my behavior and then my life.

"From that day on, that control-blackmail became part of my everyday existence and part of my relationship with my mother. The control wasn't the same every year; its intensity varied, depending on factors that didn't always have to do with me. Sometimes I thought she'd forgotten all about it, and then it would resume, as virulent as ever. In the last few years, my mother started up again about the great disgrace that had come over her, the guilt she bore for a crime she hadn't committed, and so forth. That was when she met Dona Laureta and they became friends and confidantes. Not long afterward, my mother died. I felt an amazing relief; I thought the nightmare was over.

"Then, at the seventh-day Mass, Dona Laureta came up to me in church and said that she was sad to have learned about a story—a secret, in fact—that my mother had entrusted to her. I looked at that woman without a word, trying to figure out where she was going with that. Dona Laureta said that my mother had told her that she was scared that I was plotting to kill her, and that she was sure that I would kill her soon, just like I'd killed that little girl in the Peixoto District.

"I didn't say a word, but I panicked. Not because she could have thought that about me, but because I realized that this woman was planning to extend the exploitation my mother had begun. That day, at Mass, she didn't speak to me again. But then, the first time she went to the Caixa to get her pension, she told me through the window that she couldn't bear the weight of those crimes on her conscience, that at the end of the day she wasn't my mother and she didn't have any reason to carry the moral and legal responsibility for that secret. The next month, she announced that she'd go to the police . . . unless I helped lighten the load of her guilt. And she suggested that her next pension payment be increased by twenty percent. To make the threat even more convincing, she added that she was ready to go to the police and reveal not only that I had killed my mother but that other crime I had committed when I was a boy. And she threatened to tell my superiors at the bank about my criminal history. The fear accumulated through all those years made me give in to the blackmail, and from that point on she started to receive a pension augmented by a personal contribution from me. Every time she did, she thanked me and made a discreet reference to her original threat."

At that point, Hugo Breno paused once more, got up, stretched his legs and his torso, massaged his neck, went out to the balcony, and looked out at the street. Espinosa took advantage of the pause and stretched his own body. He walked around the room, which wasn't more than four or five paces wide, and went out to join Hugo on the balcony.

"Do you want to order something to eat? A sandwich, some lunch . . ."

"I'd like a sandwich, with orange juice and coffee."

Espinosa put through Hugo's order and ordered a sandwich for himself, and while he was waiting for the lunch to arrive the conversation wandered off on an unrelated theme. Hugo Breno looked tired. Probably because of the tension of the story, though he hadn't shown any emotion while telling it. Yet it was impossible for events such as those not to leave any impression on him, Espinosa thought. Unless it had all been so thoroughly exploited by his mother for so many years that she had stripped those events of their emotional resonance. Hugo Breno was a dry man. Emotionally dry.

It didn't take long for the sandwiches to arrive. Despite a certain inevitable awkwardness, they both ate with pleasure and in no great hurry. Once the coffee was finished, they went back to the chairs and took up the conversation where they'd left it.

"How long did Dona Laureta's blackmail last?"

"From the time my mother died until her own death. A year, more or less."

"And you never met outside the bank, after your mother's Mass?"

"Never . . . until the afternoon of her death."

"What do you mean?"

"When she was in the bank that morning to get her pension, she said it was really hard for her to stand the idea that I had killed my mother and was still living in the same apartment where I'd lived with her. I said that the apartment belonged to both of us, and that now it was mine. She said that in the case of killing one's mother the child doesn't have the right to inherit, and that if I doubled my contribution she might be able to bear the pain a bit easier. I answered that I couldn't do what she asked because that would be half of my salary, and I wouldn't have enough to live on. So she said that if that was the case she would go that same afternoon to speak with the chief of the Twelfth Precinct. She made a point of saying that she'd go at five because she knew how late I got off and that way I could see how she really was going to go through with it.

"As soon as I got off work I went out to see if she really was going to do it. I saw her on the corner, as if she was waiting for me. And I really did see her go into the station. So now it was my turn to wait on the corner. But when she came out less than ten minutes later, I noticed that she hadn't managed to speak with the chief—who I knew was you. I wasn't so worried about her turning me in. That was just her own craziness. But I knew that as soon as she told you, I would have to deal with all kinds of awkward situations, giving depositions in the presence of police officers and a lawyer. And after our meeting this Monday at the station in the presence of two other officers, I could see for myself how uncomfortable an investigation could have been. That's why I suggested this meeting.

"But to get back to the story: after she left the station, I followed her. I was sure she'd go back to the station, I just didn't know if it would be that same afternoon or the next day. I ended up betting that she'd go home first to drop off her groceries, and then go back to the station. That's exactly what she did. On her way back, she stopped at a traffic light, waiting to cross the street. There were plenty of people around; that's a busy corner. People were pressed up against one another and she was standing next to the curb. I decided to give her a little scare. Just to let her know that I could pressure her, too. I didn't have any intention of hurting her. I got right up next to her ear and said in a gruff voice: 'Did your payment arrive?' As soon as she turned her face and saw me, she jumped forward. I didn't even touch her."

There was a silence that lasted a minute, or only a few seconds, but that felt very long to Espinosa.

"That's what I wanted to say," Hugo Breno concluded.

Silence once again. On Hugo Breno's part, the silence seemed definitive. For Espinosa, that silence could cover the last thirty-two years. They got up and stood facing each other for a few seconds.

"Shall we go down?" Espinosa asked.

Welber and Ramiro had obeyed the boss's orders not to go near the hotel. They'd decided to stay on a park bench—far enough away to obey the chief's orders, but close enough to intervene, if necessary—with a good view of the entrance to the hotel. They saw Espinosa and Hugo Breno come down the street toward the square and say their farewells on the corner. Welber and Ramiro went around the block and managed to get to the station one minute before Espinosa, in time to answer the call he made as soon as he went into his office.

Espinosa wanted to report the dialogue while it was still fresh in his memory. He couldn't reproduce it literally, but he wanted to recount at least what his interlocutor had said. The two listened attentively. Even summed up, it was a long story. Certain passages couldn't be condensed without losing their meaning. The chief spoke without pausing, and neither of them asked questions. Only when the story was over did Welber look at Ramiro; then the two of them asked almost simultaneously:

"And now?"

"What do you think we can do?"

"Indict him for homicide," Welber ventured.

"On what grounds? The crime of whispering into an old lady's ear? And even if that were a crime, what proof do we have that it actually happened?"

"He confessed."

"Confessed where? At the station? With witnesses? In the presence of a lawyer? Or in a hotel room, without witnesses, in an informal conversation with a policeman who had been his childhood friend? Nothing he said to me can be proven. And of course he's not going to tell the same story he told me if invited to depose. We wouldn't even manage to wrap up the investigation.

And even if we did, no judge would accept it. It wouldn't even go to court."

"Chief, he confessed to pushing the girl and he practically confessed that he killed or let his mother die, and he confessed to provoking the death of Dona Laureta. We can't do anything?"

"He didn't provoke Dona Laureta's death," Espinosa said. "There was no intent and he couldn't predict that the woman would leap forward; and he didn't confess that he killed his mother or that he let her die; she had a heart attack. As for the death of the girl, he doesn't even know if he was the one who pushed her."

"We—"

"We can't do anything."

"So that's it?"

"I don't think he's going to do anything more than keep on wandering through crowds. That is, if he can stand carrying around the guilt about the girl's death for much longer. And he no longer has his mother to share that guilt with him. We don't have anything material to incriminate him. So we can close this case, a case we never opened."

Only after the meeting with Welber and Ramiro did Espinosa notice a piece of paper underneath a stapler. It was a message from Irene, and it had been there since lunchtime: "Dona Irene called twice. She wanted to let you know that she's going to São Paulo today and will be back Monday night."

14

The weekend put the Hugo Breno case on hold. Deep down, Espinosa didn't believe that the private confession on Friday had wrapped things up. He thought it brought more of a pause than a definitive end to the events that had been opened up since Dona Laureta's death. It really wasn't a single series of events so much as two or three different intersecting incidents, but the question of Hugo Breno's involvement had been closed, even if there were a few ambiguities left over that needed to be cleared up. Espinosa knew that each event could be interpreted in several different ways, and that every one of these interpretations was, in and of itself, a different event. That was why Hugo Breno would always carry with him the weight of at least two deaths, one from his childhood and one from adulthood, both of which had their attendant interpretations. Perhaps neither was intentional, which could attenuate his guilt, even though they were real deaths—and nothing could attenuate that.

Saturday morning and afternoon were dedicated to organizing his apartment and choosing in what order to read the books that had piled up on the little table next to his rocking chair. He decided that maintaining his apartment wouldn't have to involve performing all the electrical, plumbing, and carpentry repairs that he'd planned to do; all he had to do was wash the dishes that had accumulated in the sink, take out the trash, and put his dirty clothes in the wash. He'd leave the maid to do the job of sweeping the floor and dusting the furniture, since one of his most stable relationships was with her (perhaps because he saw her only once a week . . . like Irene). At the end of the afternoon, he went out to buy some ingredients to augment his evening meal. On Sunday, his domestic program extended throughout the day, and included a meal ordered in. He missed Irene, but that would be made up for when she got back from São Paulo the next day.

As soon as he got up on Monday, he took a shower. He was making breakfast when the phone rang. He immediately thought it was Irene, saying she was getting in that afternoon, and he picked up happily. It was Ramiro, saying that Dona Adélia, Laureta's friend, with whom he'd chatted twice, had been found dead in her apartment, in the hotel where she lived.

Fifteen minutes later, Espinosa arrived at his office, where Ramiro was waiting for him.

"I got the phone call five minutes before I called you. Welber's already gone up."

"What do you know?"

"It seems she broke her neck. The manager of the hotel said that she was found on the bathroom floor, and that she had probably broken her neck when she hit the ground. The Ninth Precinct's already been alerted. The manager of the hotel knows the chief there."

"Who do we know from the Ninth?"

"Several people, including Chief Meireles."

"Let's go to the hotel."

The crime scene was as preserved as it could be. The maid, who had found the body, had called the manager, who'd found another maid there when he arrived. So at least three people had entered the room before the police got there.

Chief Meireles, two cops from the Ninth Precinct, and Welber were talking in the hallway, outside the apartment, when Espinosa arrived with Ramiro. There were no introductions, just greetings, since they all knew one another. Neither the forensic team nor the autopsy people had arrived yet, but Meireles said he suspected that Dona Adélia had been dead since the night before.

"That's just my opinion," he added.

Espinosa thought the position of the body was strange, as if it had been forced to fit into the small space into which it had fallen, between the sink and the toilet. He mentioned this to Meireles.

"We also thought it was almost impossible for some-one to fall and break their neck in this bathroom. Any-body, even an old person with slower reflexes, tries to find something to grab when they fall. And in this bath-room there are several things she could have instinc-tively reached for: the sink, the door of the shower, the towel racks, and even the toilet bowl. And even if she'd fallen straight onto the ground, there wouldn't be any space for her to hit her head in such a way that she'd break her neck."

According to the manager, it was highly possible for someone to have gone to the victim's apartment without being noticed, especially on a Sunday night, when so many people were around. He explained that many guests came to the hotel only to spend the weekend, and then returned home at the end of Sunday afternoon or on the last night flights. Besides those guests, there were some who preferred to go out on Sunday night, to dinner or a show. So a person could perfectly well walk into the hotel as if they were staying there and go up to the rooms. Once he got there, all he would have to do was ring the bell and say anything at all to get the door opened. So it was possible that someone could have gone up to the apartment, killed Dona Adélia, arranged the body so that it would look like an accident, and then left without anyone noticing.

Espinosa brought Meireles up to date on the case that, because there was no proof, hadn't even been officially investigated, and in which this victim was the last living witness. They agreed that each would conduct his own investigation, but that they would keep each other informed about the progress of their teams. They also agreed to communicate the partial results of their investigations, starting with the results of the autopsy and forensic examinations.

Espinosa, Welber, and Ramiro went back to the station. The first thing Espinosa did was finish his breakfast, which he'd started at home, and which Ramiro's phone call had interrupted.

"Now what, boss?" Inspector Ramiro asked.

"I don't know if it changes anything we already know. Unless the things we think we know aren't true. If we imagine that the death in the hotel was a crime, and that the crime was committed by Hugo Breno, that wouldn't change anything he told me in our conversation on Friday. And I think he thinks the same way, whether or not he's guilty of any of those deaths. In that case, why would he take the risk of killing someone else, when he was already sure he wouldn't be accused of any of those deaths? What would he gain from another killing?"

"He'd gain by eliminating the last witness to the things his mother told her friends," Ramiro said. "He might imagine that Dona Adélia knew more things than what he told us and so he decided to eliminate whatever was left from his past."

"Leaving in place the story he told me. Nobody else would be left to question his version."

"If that is what it is, he did a brilliant job," Welber observed.

"Then let's try to discover which of those stories was true . . . if any of them were."

It would be quite a coup, Espinosa thought. Suspected of responsibility in three deaths—the first one, he couldn't be charged for; the second, killing his mother; the third, a deliberate homicide—the criminal created a dramatic story in which he had been the victim, since

childhood, of the cruelty and religious obsession of his
mother, who died of a heart attack; then he inverted the
meaning of his mother's friend's death, so that he ended
up the persecuted victim of her blackmail; and finally he
told a dramatic story in which he described himself as
rejected by Espinosa, his childhood idol. In a word, a solitary, unhappy, hardworking, honest, and . . . innocent
man. And he, Espinosa, an experienced law enforcement officer, feeling psychologically guilty, swallowed
the whole story and let the man off. And then, to top it
all off, by an extraordinary coincidence, the only person
who could challenge his story, at least in part, turns up
dead in a hotel bathroom . . . with a broken neck.

When Hugo Breno got off work on Monday and
stepped onto the sidewalk, he found Espinosa waiting
for him. A sensitive and experienced gaze could have
captured the urge to flee that, for a fraction of a second,
he barely managed to think about. After that, his attitude bordered on the farcical.

"Chief Espinosa . . . what a pleasure. I feel like a
little kid whose older brother comes to pick him up at
school. To what do I owe this pleasant meeting?"

"To what you did last night."

"And what did I do last night?"

"Maybe you should tell me."

"I'm sure that what I did last night won't be of the

slightest interest either to Espinosa the man or to Espinosa the policeman."

"Why don't you tell me?"

"Chief, I think Sunday's the worst day of the week. Sunday offers everything I don't like and nothing I do. The morning was less unpleasant because I got through my physical exercise: I jogged and swam before all the beachcombers arrived. The afternoon was terribly boring and I didn't even leave home. At night, I watched movies on TV. Three in a row."

"Can you tell me which ones?"

"Not only which ones and who starred in them, but I can also summarize the plots. . . . Except for the last one . . . I fell asleep before the end."

"We can do that while we walk home."

"I hadn't planned to go home now, but I'll be more than happy to tell you about the films."

While they were walking, Hugo summed up the films, telling Espinosa what time they began, their plots, and how they ended (except for the last one), as if he were happily telling a friend what he'd seen on TV the night before.

"Now that I've told you about the movies, why don't you tell me what happened last night? It must have been more interesting than the movies I watched, because otherwise you wouldn't be waiting for me to get off work."

"I'm sorry, I can't say. I need one more thing: What time did you get home to start watching those films?"

"I didn't. I was already home. I only went out in the morning."

"Can you prove that?"

"Chief Espinosa, you know that I live alone, that I don't have any friends, and that I don't talk to the neighbors. And the watchman is off on Sundays."

They'd reached the corner of Barata Ribeiro and Siqueira Campos. Hugo Breno was looking in the direction of his home, as if waiting for authorization to go there.

"Do you think you're finally done with your past now?" Espinosa asked.

"A strange question, Chief, especially because I don't know what you mean by that *now*."

"Yes, you do. See you later."

Espinosa crossed Siqueira Campos and kept walking down Barata Ribeiro. Hugo Breno, instead of going up Siqueira Campos, went toward the Avenida Copacabana . . . in search of the crowd.

Espinosa's cell phone rang when he was already in the Peixoto District. It was Welber.

"Chief, we've got the news from forensics. They say it's almost impossible for her to have broken her neck in the position she was found in. The examiner thinks the body was placed in the bathroom after her neck was broken. And he thinks that the victim had been dead for at least twelve hours when the body was found; after the autopsy he'll be able to say more precisely."

"Was anything stolen? Any sign that the murderer was looking for something?"

"Nothing. There was some money in a drawer that could easily have been taken. Jewelry in a wooden box that might as well have had the word 'jewels' engraved in gold on the top. Apparently nothing was taken."

"Unless he was looking for something specific, which he would have gotten by threatening her, and then killed her to get rid of the witness. Did they find any fingerprints?"

"Lots . . . repeatedly . . . basically from the victim and the cleaning staff."

"I want you to go back to the hotel in the morning with a picture of Hugo Breno. Try everyone who was working on Sunday night. If he did it, someone must have seen him."

"Unless it wasn't him," Welber said.

"Unless it wasn't him," Espinosa repeated.

When Espinosa hung up, he was already standing before the door of his building. He had a feeling he wouldn't have a peaceful night. As soon as the thought occurred to him, he remembered that Irene had said she'd be back Monday night. And it was Monday night.

Espinosa looked at his watch. It was almost seven, and already getting dark. Irene certainly had already come back from São Paulo. He didn't even wait to get up to his apartment, calling her from his cell phone as he was walking up the stairs. A woman's voice answered.

"Irene?"

"No. Who's calling?"

"Who is this?"

"Vânia. A friend of hers."

"Vânia, is that you?"

"Espinosa?"

"Yes."

"You didn't get her message? Irene called to say she couldn't get back tonight."

"I was busy all day."

"She needed more time to wrap something up. She's going to try to come back tomorrow night. Since I had to come to Rio, she said I could stay here."

"She didn't tell me that she was going to spend the weekend in São Paulo, or that she was going to stay until tomorrow."

"She didn't know. It happened all of a sudden."

"And the thing you had to deal with, have you done it?"

"Not yet . . . I haven't managed to find the person I was looking for . . ."

Espinosa didn't say anything, waiting for her to continue the sentence she had left hanging . . .

"I have to go back to São Paulo tomorrow afternoon," Vânia added.

"If you manage to find the person you're looking for . . ."

"I did, actually. Now it's up to them."

What a difference between her impetuosity the first time and her prudent hesitation now, Espinosa thought. But he didn't want to play along. The first time had been a turn-on, but something said the second time would end badly. Besides, he didn't know exactly what the game was.

"Then good luck to you."

For the second time, Vânia had offered herself as a substitute for Irene. It was hard for Espinosa to suppose that Irene was consciously and intentionally participating in that amorous game. Unless she'd fallen in love with someone else and wanted to end their relationship by offering Vânia as a kind of consolation prize. But he clearly remembered what she'd said: "If either of us wants to end the relationship someday, all we'd need to do is say the word. We don't have to divide our property, carry away our clothes, or fetch personal mementos." That was true as far as material things went, but he didn't know how it would be to gather up or get rid of the extremely pleasurable and happy moments they'd spent together. No matter how tasty the compensation, you couldn't get rid of some things by just saying the word . . . or by quietly moving away.

Espinosa took off his clothes, took a shower, put on some comfortable house clothes, grabbed whatever was in the fridge for a possible dinner, all of which could be prepared quickly, while thinking about what was happening between him, Irene, and Vânia. He didn't even know if Irene's supposed participation in the drama was real or just a fantasy he had cooked up as an excuse for his immediate, voluntary acceptance of Vânia's first proposition.

An hour later, seated in his rocking chair with a book in his lap, he was still feeling perplexed by everything that was going on, and unhappy with himself. Feelings he'd been having for the last two or three weeks. Espinosa opened the book to where he'd left off, but immediately had to go back a few pages to remember what had happened before.

Tuesday morning. Welber had gone to the hotel to see if anyone recognized Hugo Breno. Espinosa and Ramiro were talking in the boss's office.

"How was your conversation with Hugo Breno yesterday?" Ramiro asked.

"He said he spent Sunday night watching TV movies. He gave me the times, the titles, and the plot of every one of them, and then summed them all up for me. A bit too detailed to be true. He might have read about them in the TV guide, or he could have taped whatever was on that night . . ."

"Did you pressure him?"

"Not explicitly. He's either innocent or he's very clever. He wanted me to tell him why I was investigating, but I didn't give him any clues about what we're looking into. He's going to try to find out what it's all about."

"Chief, if he's guilty, he's just closed the circle: all the witnesses to his past are dead . . . except for you."

"I'm not a witness to his past—we were just kids who lived in the same neighborhood. I didn't even remember him at first."

"But you managed to gather enough material so that you could, together with his own story, piece together the places where he was involved in someone's death."

"What are you insinuating with that?"

"Exactly what you're thinking."

"Come out with it, Ramiro."

"I'm suggesting that you might be the next, and last, element in the series. It's not a crazy idea. I'd suggest that you pay close attention and deal with him very carefully."

"In that case, he'd have to kill you and Welber, since he knows that you know all about him."

"But we're not witnesses to anything, we've just heard what you told us. We aren't significant to him. His own personal drama wouldn't change a bit if we were dead. I think he wants you, sir."

Ever since Friday in the hotel in the Peixoto District, when he'd heard Hugo Breno's tale, Espinosa had

had the feeling that he was not only a confidant, but an integral part of the story. And not just a part of an obscure, far-off episode, but a key to a whole life history. It made sense that the final reckoning would be with him.

"Ramiro, this isn't the end of a real story, it's the end of a delirium. The Espinosa in his story is a fantasy, not a real person."

"All right, Chief, but if he wants to fire at that fantasy, you'll be the one who dies."

At noon Welber arrived with the news that nobody at Dona Adélia's hotel had recognized Hugo Breno in the picture he'd shown them.

"He's got a distinctive face and thick bushy hair, which means that any alteration to his face would leave him unrecognizable," said Welber, who was an expert on disguise.

The three of them went out to lunch together, something they did less and less since Selma had started keeping an eye on Welber's diet and Ramiro had decided to start economizing. But the lunch at the trattoria was still feasible for all three of them, especially during the first couple of weeks of the month.

On the way, Ramiro talked to Welber about the conversation he'd had with Espinosa, and about the threat Hugo Breno might pose to the chief.

"After so many twists and turns, I have to say I no longer know what to think of that man," Welber said. "I think that everything we're putting on him really might just be our imaginations, like the boss says. Maybe it's been our imagination from the beginning, ours along with the two old ladies', way more than real facts."

"We're not inventing those deaths," Espinosa interrupted. "They actually happened, so this last one is more than suspicious. And suspecting Hugo Breno is not just pure fantasy on our part. We can't keep trying to decide between full guilt and total innocence. I think the girl's death, thirty-two years ago, just like Hugo's mother's death, can be considered accidents. But Dona Laureta's death and Dona Adélia's, on the other hand, can be considered intentional."

As soon as they went into the restaurant, they changed the subject.

15

The autopsy information, transmitted by Meireles by telephone, indicated as a possible cause of death a break in the cervical column.

"Compatible with what happens in a fall," Meireles commented. "Everything indicates that the old lady broke her neck in a fall. And we were already tying the noose around your suspect. . . . But the guy who did the autopsy wanted to make sure I said that this wasn't a definitive result."

Espinosa didn't expect the final verdict to change the original finding, that the death was the result of a fall. From what Meireles told him, the cause of death was not asphyxia or a twist of the head, common forms of criminal homicide, but a kind of fracture that frequently occurs in falls. That wouldn't exclude the hypothesis of murder, it would just require that the murderer have specific training and enough sangfroid to simulate an accidental fracture. Hugo Breno followed a rigid military discipline when it came to his physical preparation; Espinosa wondered if that preparation included learning ways to kill without recourse to arms.

Yet Espinosa's suspicion didn't match the pathetic private story of a solitary man who apparently required psychiatric attention more than a police investigation.

That afternoon, after his usual meeting with his team, Espinosa decided to walk home via the longer route. He needed to let his ideas flow freely, without the pressure imposed by the station.

Carried along by this flow of ideas, Espinosa's steps sped up or slowed down depending on how fast they came into his mind. At some points, the chief slowed down so much that he almost stopped, in an effort to articulate ideas and images that were apparently irreconcilable. He'd already considered the possibility that the case of Hugo Breno had moved from the police realm into the personal sphere, with the conversation in the hotel being the latest sign of that shift. That was nothing new. Whether or not the whole conversation in the hotel had been set up by Hugo, the question of how far he had been willing to go just to meet Espinosa didn't remove his own reservations. In the absence of proof or even of concrete signs of Hugo Breno's involvement in any of those deaths, there wasn't even the possibility of initiating an official inquiry. His preliminary investigations had been inconclusive. Reduced to the two participants, the case would soon, once again, be nothing more than something in two people's memories. The meeting in the Peixoto District hotel had not only been an extrajudicial deposition, it had nothing to do with the police case being investigated, at least not directly; the police investigation had done nothing more than bring about the first meeting between them in more than thirty years. Espinosa thought that this figure meant two different things to Hugo Breno and himself. The impression he'd gotten after their conversation in the hotel was that for Hugo Breno, that Friday and their games in the square were one and the same present tense, not two distant moments separated by decades. Those years of distant contact with Espinosa in the neighborhood park, when Hugo was eleven, and his contact with him now, when he was past forty, were, for Hugo, a circle that was about to close. It was as if the early years were the first words of a sentence that was about to be given its last word, the word that would give the whole phrase its meaning. So Hugo Breno wouldn't be in the least worried about eliminating witnesses or anything else (a simple police matter); he would concentrate on preparing the final act.

That was the useful portion of the ideas that were floating through his brain as Espinosa returned home. He thought that they were useful only to the extent that they formed a nexus, not because they revealed the enigma of a life. Just ideas, he thought as he crossed the square.

Only once he was already in front of his building did he see Irene seated on the steps in front of the door. He sat next to her and neither said anything for a short while, her head resting on his shoulder.

"Shall we go up?" Espinosa proposed, taking her hands and helping her up.

"I didn't bring anything to eat or drink," she said.

"We'll call and order something. Until it arrives, we can act like cannibals."

The next morning, the e-mail Meireles sent to Espinosa turned the case on its head once again. All it said was: "The autopsy confirms that the cause of death was a break in the spinal cord, but added this morning was that the woman was already dead when she fell in the bathroom. Best, Meireles." Espinosa, Ramiro, and Welber looked at the message on the screen, perplexed.

"So are we back where we started?" Ramiro asked.

"So the cause of death . . ." Welber babbled.

"The cause of death was the break in her neck. Except that that happened before her fall. In other words, someone broke the poor woman's neck and then arranged her body on the floor of the bathroom to give the impression that she had died in a fall," said Espinosa.

"Hugo Breno," Welber suggested, still puzzled.

"Not necessarily," said Espinosa. "You can't conclude that 'the woman was already dead when she fell in the bathroom' has to mean that the murderer was Hugo Breno. That's much more an expression of our own desires than the logical conclusion. Let's be careful not to get into dangerous speculations."

"So you think Hugo Breno wouldn't have wanted to make his life more complicated with this new twist?"

"How would it change his situation?"

"He doesn't have an alibi."

"He has the same one he had before."

"But he can't prove it."

"You don't need to prove that you were home watching TV on a Sunday night. Besides, he gave the names of the movies he watched, described the three stories in detail, told me the names of the actors. . . . Of course he could have taped them. The problem is that I don't know if he has a recorder that could tape three full-length films."

"There are other ways."

"Fine. I'm not saying it wasn't him, I'm just trying to show that we don't have any way to prove that it was him. And that's why I'm saying that his situation hasn't changed since last week."

"What are we going to do? Wait for him to fess up voluntarily?"

"That's not out of the question. We just need some bait."

"What kind of bait?"

"Me, for instance."

"Chief—"

"If you really think that he was the one who killed Dona Adélia, you must have noticed that in that case he's changed his tactics radically. For the first time he would have committed a deliberate murder. If we believe the story he told me, the previous victims died without his intentionally and directly causing their deaths. The death of Dona Adélia, though, would be the first instance of a crime he planned and carried out with the precision of a professional killer. I even thought that he might have been the intellectual author of the crime and that he'd hired someone else to carry it out. He doesn't consider himself a murderer. It'd make sense if he'd hired someone. But I changed my mind. He's essentially a loner who acts alone; he wouldn't want to join forces with someone else."

"And why would he have killed Dona Adélia?"

"In his mind, it wouldn't be a murder. For him, the important thing isn't Dona Adélia, but her function. The same thing goes for Dona Laureta. That man, when he was a child, imagined a destiny for himself that opposed the one planned for him by his mother, who thought that her son was possessed by evil. His mother, Dona Laureta, and Dona Adélia play a role and have a function in this delirious construction. He doesn't see himself as a murderer. He's just living out his destiny."

"And what is your role in that delirium?"

"I represent good. By identifying with me, which is to say with good, he can escape the figure of evil that inhabits him."

"Chief," Ramiro asked, "where did you pull all this out of?"

"From my head. Where else?"

"You mean that none of it is based on reality?"

"All the characters are real. And they're all, more or less, the way Hugo sees them."

"Then why don't we have him put into a psychiatric hospital?"

"Because just like it's not always easy to prove that someone's a criminal, it's not always easy to prove that someone's crazy."

Espinosa didn't tell his two colleagues what he himself really thought about the murder of Dona Adélia in the hotel. If her death eliminated the last witness to Hugo Breno's past, that death also wrapped up the investigation into his hypothetical guilt. Case closed, the cops would say, and now we don't have any other way to get him. He'd be free from Espinosa's persecution. And that was exactly what Hugo Breno didn't want to happen. After more than three decades, he'd managed to meet up with Espinosa. . . . They'd spent almost an entire day talking in a hotel room. . . . Espinosa had gone to see him at the bank and then waited for him when he was coming off work. . . . Hugo wouldn't want to move away from Espinosa now that the investigation had been closed. Hugo wouldn't allow that to happen, Espinosa thought. If necessary, he'd confess to a crime just to keep up a relationship with Espinosa, so as not to lose the connection he'd waited for through so many long decades.

He thought it was excessive to get into all that with his

two associates, when both Welber and Ramiro had found his interpretation of Hugo Breno's delirium strange and overdone. For now, the best thing to do was wait. If he was right, the next move would be Hugo's, at which point he might try a more radical approach.

On Thursday, there was a market in the square in the Peixoto District, which Espinosa visited to stock up on fruits and vegetables. It was also the day when he could gauge his popularity from the greetings he got during his walk through the market and the eagerness with which the vendors tried to help him. Despite his reserved character, the chief thought it was pleasant to be greeted that warmly by the neighborhood residents.

Espinosa had walked all around the square, done his shopping, and was getting ready to take his purchases home when he saw Hugo Breno coming toward him. That wasn't the person he had wanted to meet that early in the morning, before he'd even gone in to the station. From what Welber and Ramiro had told him about Hugo Breno, at that hour he must have already run up and down the entire length of Copacabana Beach, finished his swim, gone home, taken a shower, and . . . here he was, ready for his encounter with Espinosa. He was carrying a bag with a few groceries. Not much. Probably just enough to justify his presence at the market, at the same hour, when they had never seen each other there before. Or maybe they had, several times, though Espinosa had never noticed the resemblance between that man and the boy he'd seen countless times in that same square, when he too was a child.

"Chief Espinosa, good morning. What a nice surprise!"

"Good morning."

"What a special day. The first time we've run into each other here, buying food for our solitary meals. The only thing that keeps us from being twins is that your Friday night meals aren't solitary like mine. Good for you. I hope we see each other again. It really was a pleasure. See you."

Hugo Breno said this and walked off, as if he'd delivered that short speech on somebody's orders.

Espinosa didn't like it. First, because there was nothing casual about it: he'd never before seen Hugo Breno at the market. Second, for the elaborate, excessive politeness. It wasn't like Hugo. In fact, it was the opposite of him. So why had he gone to such lengths to be so polite? It could only be to send a message: I know about your habits and when you come and go; I know that you're by yourself, except on Friday nights, when your girlfriend has dinner and sleeps over with you in your apartment. Espinosa didn't like that one bit. He considered it an invasion of privacy, though an open market couldn't be considered a private space. He went up to his apartment, left his purchases in the kitchen, went into the living room, opened one of the windows, and scanned the whole perimeter of the square. Not a sign of Hugo Breno. He waited a few minutes and then went back down.

At the station, he mentioned the encounter to Welber and Ramiro.

"He turned up earlier than I'd expected," Ramiro said.

"What could that mean?" Welber asked.

"It might mean that he's more nervous than we are," Espinosa answered.

With that in mind, they decided that the best thing to do would be to make clear to Hugo Breno that Chief Espinosa was no longer interested in him.

"That means that we're not going to do anything at all," said Espinosa. "Nothing that he can see, of course."

That same morning, shortly after ten, Welber got a call from his house. It was Selma telling him happily that they'd received a gift of a fruit basket from the market vendors in the Peixoto District. A note welcomed Detective Welber and his wife. Welber immediately passed on the news to Ramiro and Espinosa.

"It was him! That piece of shit was in my building."

"He delivered it himself?" Espinosa asked.

"No. He left it with the doorman."

"Try to remain calm. Any slight sign of nervousness on our part would be a point for him. The more indifferently we act, the more he'll feel weak and unprotected. It's a face-off. The winner is whoever resists longer."

"My resistance ends the moment he sticks his nose into my home," said Welber.

"He knows what your limits are," Espinosa observed.

"And if he doesn't lay off?"

"Then we'll let him know we think he's annoying."

"That's it?"

"That, for him, is everything."

There were times when Espinosa had the idea that he was doing exactly the opposite of what a law enforcement officer ought to be doing. Not deliberately, based on clear ideas or a firm decision. And that was the problem. Sometimes he felt like he was being blown along by events that escaped any means of prediction or control. For Hugo Breno, killing a defenseless old lady who hadn't done anything at all to him wasn't a criminal act, just like it wasn't a criminal act to kill an enemy in battle. For someone who thought along those lines, homicide was not necessarily judged according to what was good or evil, but according to what was permitted and what was forbidden, or even according to aesthetic criteria, as in a struggle between warriors. After that thought, Espinosa wondered if Hugo Breno wouldn't be able to kill someone just to "stay in touch." In that case, how much would Espinosa himself be strengthening that perverse logic in Hugo Breno's mind? If he thought of it that way, the decision not to do anything for a while might not be correct, or even very prudent.

Espinosa chose a sandwich and a fruit juice at the bar across the street. Out of pure lack of initiative, not because he was expecting something important or imminent to occur. Sometimes his daily life was taken over by a generalized lack of interest, but that rarely lasted for more than part of a day. It never lingered into the next.

At the end of the day, before he went home, Espinosa called Welber and Ramiro into his office. The two were the only cops involved in the case and Espinosa wanted to warn them of possible actions Hugo Breno might take.

"Be prepared not only for violence, but also for little things like what he did this morning, designed just to irritate and provoke us. You should only react if he resorts to physical violence against you or others. Warn your families about these friendly, seductive deliveries."

On his way home, he decided to call Irene in order to warn her about Hugo Breno as well and temporarily suspend her visits to his apartment in the Peixoto District. It would be better for them to meet at her place or somewhere else.

Irene told him that morning she had received a dozen white roses, with an electronically printed card that said: "Sorry we can't meet tomorrow. Love, Espinosa."

"I didn't send you flowers . . ."

"I didn't think so. Who did?"

"That guy who likes crowds."

"And how does he know about our meeting tomorrow?"

"He knows that we meet here on Fridays. He spies on my apartment. He knows my routines. From the square, he watches the living-room window."

"Who is this person? What does he want?"

"His name is Hugo Breno. He wants to be my friend . . ."

"He wants to be your friend and he's spying on you? For how long?"

"Apparently, since we were kids."

"Since . . . ! Is he sick?"

"Maybe. That's better than the other possibility."

"Which is?"

"That he might have committed a few murders."

"Might have or did?"

"We're still not sure about that."

"And there's no proof? Do you think you're going to find any?"

"I think so. It won't be long. Maybe as soon as the end of the week. Until then, I want you to be extra careful. Only take official taxis, and when you call, ask for a driver you know. Tomorrow, avoid going out in the neighborhood on foot. Keep your cell phone close by and always have it on. I'll give you Welber's cell number. If you have to go out on foot, call him."

"Honey, you're not overdoing it?"

"I hope so. Do you have anything tomorrow?"

"I have an important meeting at an advertising agency in Botafogo."

"I'll send Welber with you."

"It might be a long meeting. Is he just going to sit there waiting for me?"

"That doesn't matter. He's used to long waits, and in much less pleasant places."

16

Friday morning. Welber was assigned to protect Irene and Ramiro was going to track Hugo Breno in the morning, before he went to work, and in the evening, after he got off. Espinosa didn't like the note Irene had received, in his own name, calling off their meeting. He didn't like the white roses either. He might be over-doing it, as Irene had said, with his precautions as well as in the ways he interpreted the facts, but he felt that Hugo Breno had changed his pattern of behavior. He'd become more daring, more flashy in his intentions and actions, and Espinosa didn't want to be taken by surprise.

He spent the morning and the afternoon handling the most bureaucratic and uninteresting tasks in the life of a police chief. It was one of the most efficient ways to turn off the outside world and transport him-self into the world of papers and the computer screen. Even so, every phone call provoked a mixture of dis-comfort and fear. Luckily, as if obeying a secret com-mand of his, he got very few phone calls. It wasn't until five-twenty that his cell phone rang. It was Ramiro.

"Chief, Hugo Breno's not at the bank, he's at home."

"Home?"

"I got to the front of the bank at four-thirty, waiting

for him to come out. When he hadn't come out by five-ten, I called the security guard and went in. He wasn't there. A coworker said that he hadn't felt well and had left earlier. I went to his building, rang the doorbell, and the watchman said that he'd gotten back around four and hadn't gone out since. I crossed the street and sat watching the sidewalk in front. After a few minutes, he turned up at the window and closed the curtains. The watchman told me that that was his bedroom window. Now I'm down here waiting for him to come out, but it doesn't seem like he's going to."

Ramiro called back at six-thirty.

"Chief, I think he went to sleep. There's only a weak light on in the bedroom. It must be the bedside lamp. The rest of the apartment is dark."

"Wait another half hour. If it doesn't seem like he's going to go out, you can go home. Did you talk to Welber?"

"I did. He's in the waiting room of a firm in Botafogo. Dona Irene's been in a meeting for more than two hours. The secretary said that the meeting might last another half hour."

"Fine. I'm going home. If you need to speak to me, call my cell."

It was seven when Espinosa left the station. He told the operator to transfer all personal calls to his cell phone and went home. At that hour, it was getting dark, the sidewalks were still packed, and the traffic along Barata Ribeiro was slow. Since he was on foot, he'd be home in a few minutes. He'd have time to shower, get dressed, and pick Irene up at nine.

Welber had already flipped through all the foreign magazines on the coffee table in the waiting room of the ad agency, all of which included pictures of furniture and objects from Scandinavia, Germany, the United States, and Italy, things he had never seen and probably never would, except in photographs. At seven-ten, Ramiro called to tell him about Hugo Breno. They both agreed that they could go home as soon as Irene's meeting was over. He kept on flipping through a magazine, but the images started growing fuzzy, until he suddenly darted out of the chair, grabbed his phone, and called Ramiro.

"Ramiro, are you sure that Hugo Breno's at home asleep?"

"I don't know if he's asleep, but I know he's home. I'm in front of the only door to the building, and ever since he appeared in the window nobody's come out of that door."

"Ramiro, this is all really weird to me. You'd better check to make sure he really is in the apartment."

"I'll go see. The building only has one exit: the one

right in front of me. Unless he went out through the service area and jumped over the back wall. . . . I'll call you in a minute."

Ramiro went up to the corner and walked up the short stretch of the Rua Santa Margarida until he reached the back of the building. He jumped over the wall into the service area of Hugo Breno's apartment. The door that led into the kitchen was unlocked. He went in, and in a few seconds he'd gone through the apartment. Nobody. He immediately called Welber.

"Welber, he ran off. That whole thing about the presents, flowers, that note for Irene was just to distract us. He got rid of both of us and now he's alone with Espinosa. Where's the boss?"

"I talked to him a few minutes ago. He was going home. He must be getting there now."

"He's going to get the chief! Let's go!"

Welber told the secretary of the ad agency to tell Irene not to wait for him and to go straight home. Within a minute, the detective was in a cab with his police ID in his hand, ordering the driver to go to the Peixoto District as quickly as possible. He called Espinosa's cell phone. Nobody answered.

Ramiro left Hugo Breno's building and walked the two blocks to the Peixoto District wondering if he could get there in time to prevent Hugo Breno's encounter with Espinosa. He made it to the square in less than a minute; Espinosa usually approached from the other side. To the contrary of what he expected at that hour, there were still people in the square. A group of boys were talking near the fence surrounding the soccer field; there were people sitting on the benches, boys running after a ball near the playground, a candy vendor, an ice-cream seller, people coming home after work. A few feet away, two city security guards were talking. Ramiro didn't see the boss or Hugo Breno. There was no more light in the sky and the illumination of the square was less than optimal because the lamps were partially blocked by the trees. It was impossible to see the entire square. It was about eighty meters from the place he was standing to the end of the square, and between the two points were the soccer field fence, the playground, and an enormous fountain, almost in the middle of the square, along with trees and bushes. Espinosa and Hugo Breno could be hidden behind any of those barriers. Ramiro moved slowly, concentrating as best he could on everyone he saw and their movements, searching for a point where he could see the entirety of the other side of the square.

Espinosa entered the Peixoto District coming from the Rua Anita Garibaldi. As usual, he walked down the left side of the street and started to cross the square diagonally, heading toward his building. He'd gone around the fountain and felt like he was almost home when he saw Hugo Breno coming toward him. There was no doubt that Hugo was deliberately walking over to meet him. He walked unhurriedly and was carrying a bag. Espinosa wondered if he hadn't been waiting for him on one of the benches, carrying in the sack some gift, like the ones he'd distributed yesterday. Maybe some of the Middle Eastern food he would know Espinosa liked. Yet as Hugo Breno approached, Espinosa saw that his expression was no longer happy and smiling, as it had been the morning before, when they'd met at the market. Both of them were on the paved part of the square, next to the series of benches lined up along the sidewalk.

Espinosa didn't veer from his path or alter his pace. When they were three steps away from each other, the bag fell from Hugo Breno's hand without his making the least attempt to recover it, as if he'd tossed it to the ground on purpose. Espinosa looked at his hand . . . it was holding a knife. He immediately reached back to grab his gun, even as he tried to get out of the way to avoid the blow. The knife entered him on the left side of his body, with enormous violence. Espinosa had managed to get out his gun and fire, but the shot was too low, hitting the thigh of Hugo Breno, who fell to his knees. Espinosa took one step and fell onto a wooden bench, sliding down the curved back until he reached the seat. Hugo Breno was seated on the ground, next to the same bench, with his knife still in his hand, his pants drenched with blood. Espinosa's pistol had fallen to the ground, within reach of both of them. With his shirt, Espinosa tried to stanch the bleeding from his wound. He couldn't breathe, and his vision was hazy, and he had to make an enormous effort not to close his eyes. That was when he saw Hugo Breno seated at his side, one of his hands trying to prevent the bleeding in his leg and the other reaching out toward Espinosa. Espinosa's blurry vision couldn't make out exactly what Hugo was trying to do, until he saw that Hugo's hand was holding the gun he had picked up off the ground. The other man seemed to be saying something, but the sounds reached the chief's ears blunted and indistinct, and his hazy vision only allowed him to see the movement of Hugo's lips. Espinosa didn't have the strength to move his body, much less to attempt any defense. He felt that he was about to faint when he heard a cry that seemed to come from far off in the distance. Ramiro. He couldn't see the inspector, but he saw the weapon in Hugo's hand turn against Hugo himself. Ramiro fired. Hugo Breno fired at the same time.

He woke up with a dry mouth, feeling pain when he tried to move and seeing tubes and wires hooked up to his arms. He was obviously in a hospital room. Still a bit confused, he heard Irene's voice.

"Morning, darling. Welcome back to the world!"

Irene got up from the chair beside the bed, bent over

him carefully, and gave him a kiss. Espinosa felt his dry lips.

"I'm going to wet down your mouth. It's dry."

"I'm thirsty," Espinosa managed to say.

Irene pressed the call button for a nurse.

"It hurts. . . . What happened?" His voice was hoarse and his tongue was still rough.

"You were wounded."

"I know. What happened to me?"

"They operated on you. The knife went in on your left side, from bottom to top, and perforated your lung. You'll be fine, but they had to operate to sew you up. Now you're in a special post-op room. I think that's what it's called, and the surgery went well."

"Is my lung still there?"

"One next to the other, as always. But you lost a lot of blood."

"Was Ramiro wounded? I heard him scream . . ."

"No. He and Welber spent the night here at the hospital. They went home to shower and change clothes. All I know is that Welber got to the square right after the shots were fired. As soon as one of them gets here, they'll fill you in. I came straight from home; I didn't even go by the square."

"What time is it?"

"Almost noon on Saturday."

"What kind of shape am I in?"

"You'll be here for a few days and it'll be a while before you and I can lie on top of each other again."

"We'll figure out a way."

The nurse came in, together with a doctor.

"So, Chief, pretty busy night," the doctor said.

"How am I doing, Doctor?"

"You've got a perforated lung, but we've put it back together. You had major surgery. But now you're in no more danger than if you'd had a tooth pulled. With the difference, of course, that you can chew whatever you want. On the other hand, you can't move. Your recovery will take longer than if the weapon had only gotten the muscles. In the next few days, you're going to feel pain whenever you move your torso and you're going to have a hard time walking. Try to avoid coughing, sneezing, and laughing."

"What do I have to laugh about, Doctor?"

"The fact that the knife didn't go a few centimeters higher."

"What's a few centimeters higher?"

"Your heart."

The doctor had finished examining Espinosa when Ramiro arrived. Five minutes later, Welber came in with a bouquet.

"The flowers are from everyone at the station. Everyone wanted to come with me, but I convinced them to come later, in smaller groups."

Irene took advantage of their arrival to stop by her

apartment. She hadn't been outside that room since the previous night. She agreed to come back at the end of the afternoon to spend the night with Espinosa.

When the three of them were alone, the chief asked Welber to make sure they wouldn't be interrupted. The detective saw a little door sign reading VISITS PROHIBITED and hung it outside. Espinosa asked them to tell him, once and for all, what had happened.

Ramiro and Welber explained to the boss how they had realized that they'd been tricked by Hugo Breno and how they'd then dashed to the Peixoto District. Since Ramiro was only two blocks from the square, he'd gotten there in time to see Hugo Breno attack Espinosa with a knife, to hear the shot the chief fired, and to see both of them fall side by side. Up until that point, Espinosa hadn't asked about Hugo Breno.

"He's dead, Chief. Three shots," said Ramiro. "Yours hit his femoral artery, so that he would have lost all his blood through that hole; mine pierced his thorax diagonally; and his own went straight through his heart. Any one of those shots would have killed him. I don't understand why he shot himself, if his idea was to kill you, sir. He could have fired at you right when he was pointing the gun at your head. I thought he was going to fire, so I shot him. I was surprised when I saw that he'd pointed his gun at himself. But by then I'd already fired. We both shot him practically at the same time."

"I don't know if he really wanted to kill me just then," Espinosa said, speaking softly so as not to force his breathing. "I think that when he saw me fading away on the park bench, he thought that I was dying. That was when he pointed the gun at me and ordered me to open my eyes. That was the only thing I heard him say. I don't think he wanted to shoot me. He wanted me to see him kill himself. That was probably how he imagined the final scene.... That's what I think, anyway. He was writing his own play."

"It might not have been the best ending, but..." Ramiro said.

"... but it could have been worse," Welber finished.

For a few seconds they sat there in silence.

"Play's over," Espinosa said. "Time for me to leave the scene myself."

ABOUT THE AUTHOR

A distinguished academic, LUIZ ALFREDO GARCIA-ROZA is a bestselling novelist who lives in Rio de Janeiro. His Inspector Espinosa mysteries—*The Silence of the Rain, December Heat, Southwesterly Wind, A Window in Copacabana, Pursuit,* and *Blackout*—have been translated into six languages and are available in paperback from Picador.